Sweet Blackmail

Catherine Rose

Copyright © 2015 Catherine Rose

All rights reserved.

ISBN-13: 978-1511969260

ISBN-10: 1511969261

:

DEDICATION

To all those that enjoy a little trip down fantasy lane once in awhile. May you always relish the journey..

Thank you for respecting the hard work of this author. Please note this is a work of fiction any resemblance to persons living or dead is purely coincidental. All characters engaged in sexual acts within this work of fiction are stated to be eighteen years of age or older. Cover art by Catherine Rose. All rights reserved. Except for brief passages quoted in reviews, newspapers, or other media no part of this book may be reproduced by any means without permission of the publisher.

CHAPTER 1

Eddie Harris folded his tall but lithe and muscular frame into the brand new Viper, started the motor, jerked it into reverse and pushed the machine like a rocket down the drive into the quiet street. Tires squealing and the engine revving like mad, he headed toward Third Avenue and back to the club. The ache in his balls and his feeling of sexual deprivation told him, only too clearly that there was a big void in his married life although in almost every other direction, his life had changed for the better. Jesus Christ! Jenna looks she'd be the most fabulous lay of the century... that luscious body, it sure fooled me. Why does she just lay there like a sack of flour when I fuck her? She's so Goddamn passive, I feel like I might as well shove my cock into an inflatable doll. It's not normal. She thinks everything but the missionary position is only for perverts. All she ever does is lay there and throw her legs up and wait for me to get it over with. She's so damn frosty you would think she hates me. Sighing with regret he was wondering if he'd made a terrible mistake. I better keep my mind on the road, he suddenly realized after roaring through a stop sign. He was damn lucky there was little traffic or he could have ended this night on a sour note. He needed to pay attention or risk waking up dead which would suck a lot more than divorced.

Once he got off these sleepy roads running past dark houses hidden behind walls or vaults of trees the odds are he'd be like every other driver; in a hurry and not happy about it. But presently his attention was focused back in his groin. Fuck! I've got such an ache in my balls! I didn't have to go home for dinner. I like to see my wife but apparently she isn't that happy to see me. You would think she would be thrilled that I raced home to spend a little time with her but- No; she was all pissy like he was interrupting her! He let his mind drift back over the little scene he had just gone through. Still in his hand-ball gear, he had bounced into the house, entering the kitchen where Jenna was preparing dinner for one. He enveloped his wife of three months in a gentle hug, giving her a lingering kiss, hard on her upturned lips, leaning his head down to her and using his tongue to force open her lips to him.

The chilly new bride had made this concession to her husband although she was not entirely happy about it. She believed that his desire for what she considered unnecessary sexual contact, especially, in a casual kiss of greeting or goodbye outside of the bedroom to be tacky. Jenna frowned on any type of PDA also know as by her as 'predatory displays of affection.' The lovely blonde was a little repulsed, but she had decided that it was a small thing for her to do if it was something that Eddie really wanted.

"What's on the menu, darling?" he asked, looking around the kitchen.

"Tuna salad and why are you here? Don't you have a client dinner?"

Without taking a breath she continued on changing the subject so fast that sometimes he wondered how he didn't get mental whiplash from listening to her as she said, "we're going to go strictly low calorie around here."

"Sounds great to me," he said, "those five pounds I put on over our honeymoon sure show up when I'm playing. I think it was all those chocolate éclairs for breakfast."

"Yes," she answered with mock sternness, "no more decadence at the table. I don't want this body looking like someone blew me up with a bicycle pump."

"I'd like to pump you right now," he leered at her in a suggestive manner. His hands made suggestive motions down her back, as he smoothed them across her buttocks, reveling in their firm protuberance, cupping the rounded mounds of them in his huge hand and pulling her pelvis in hard to his now stiffening prick beneath his grey sweaty shorts. Jenna could feel the warmth and the bulging, warm firmness at his crotch, and she knew that he wanted her. She could hardly stand the thought of having sex in so early the evening and she knew that he felt that it was an added extra with his dinner break.

"Don't you that meeting in two hours," she asked hopefully. "I mean you won't have time." Then she sniffed and pulled away, "and darling I would suggest a shower would be a better use of your time. You smell like a locker room."

"Baby, I've always got time for a good fuck. We could go right over there by the sink and I bend you over for a quickie. Come on baby…help your man out."

He tried again when she wouldn't respond by giving her a playful slap on the ass, as she turned to the counter to begin serving the dinner she had prepared for self. Ignoring his lewd comments she said, "You had better take a shower Eddie or you'll be late."

The sway of her hips, as she walked away from him, held his attention, his eyes riveted on her, watching the undulating flesh inside the jeans, mentally undressing her and he liked what he saw. That was the reason he had finally gotten married. This woman seemingly had everything. She looked and acted like a future law firms partners wife should in public but in private? He was already having regrets.

"I wish it was your cunt I was eating instead!"

Jenna shot him a look back over her shoulder at him. She saw her husband's lust-filled eyes, as he watched her, and she wished that she could learn how to handle Eddie's sexually suggestive innuendoes and lewd interjections.

She turned away from her husband, embarrassed, in spite of herself, the beginnings of a frown creasing her pale face as Eddie left the kitchen and headed for the bathroom. The things he says! That look of his when he wants to make love to me which he wants twenty-four hours a day, is pure lust! It's pure animal lust and it makes me feel crawly and dirty. I wish I could learn to understand it, to respond to his lewd demands, or any rate to reply without blushing to his comments. She finished setting the table and called him to the kitchen.

"I was thinking you might like to have this so you don't fill up on anything too rich at the restaurant later."

Eddie glanced once over the paltry tuna salad and said, "Since there are no sweets at the table I think I'd like you for dessert."

Saying nothing but wrinkling her nose in disgust she moved to escape him, trying to pick up some dishes from the table as a distraction. He rose, swooped and captured her easily holding her immobile in a vise-like grip, the dishes falling back to the table with a clatter. His lips sought hers and he kissed her hard and long. Finally, she placed both her hands on his chest and pushed him away from her.

"Come on, baby, give me a little bit."

"Eddie, please it's not even full dark outside yet; not even the end of the day. It just doesn't seem right somehow."

"Right. If it feels right what does the time have to do with it? I want to fuck. I'm not going to wait for the darkness."

"Well... I do feel better about it... at night, darling."

Undiscouraged, he again bent his head down to her, capturing her full lips and he was kissing her long and passionately, probing her mouth with his tongue, his hands busy on her body, exploring the womanly curves of her, kneading and caressing her, trying to communicate his great need of her through action.

The big man's fingers found the zipper on her jeans. Fearfully she heard the scraping whisper of the fastener as he opened it and the garment fell with a sigh of the material, sliding down over the swell of her hips to land in gathers around her trim ankles. She broke the kiss pulling her head back to one side.

"Eddie! What will our neighbors think?"

"The neighbors! Do you think that they have nothing better to do than to watch us?" he said, vehemently, as he dipped his hands under the elastic waistband of her panties to grasp a smoothly rounded buttock cheek in either hand.

She persisted. "But what if someone did see us through the window without our clothes. My God! What if somebody out walking their dog glances and see's us lit up in here like we are on display. Eddie, it just wouldn't be right."

Desperate to convince her he continued with greater emphasis, "Listen, we're husband and wife and this is our home. I'll do what I want in it and when I want to. No one's going to stop me. Why are you so concerned what other people think? It's our life, not theirs so why don't you just get over yourself."

Then, with a deft movement he pushed her panties down over the smooth, rounded curves of her buttocks, and the wisp of nylon joined her jeans at her ankles. The clasp of her bra occupied his attention only momentarily. He flung the garments from her, and she stood, nude, statuesque and magnificent in the middle of the kitchen, leaning into his tanned arms, pliant and unresisting. Her heated face flushed with the shame of it. Imagine being stripped naked during the dinner hour right there in the kitchen with the curtains opened.

She thought of making another complaint but she bit her tongue deciding that she would only irritate her husband more by nagging about his unseemly behavior. It seemed to her that she was always on the defensive and she didn't want Eddie to think that she objected to everything all the time although in their short marriage it was beginning to look like she did. "Oh baby, I want you. I want to fuck you now. You turn me on so much!"

His muscular arms swept her up; lifting her, easily, he carried her to their bedroom, leaving the trail of her clothing behind them on the way. He deposited his wife on the soft yielding mattress and stepped back to kick off his shoes. He clawed his gym garb from his body, frantically, scattering it about the room in a flurry of quick movements for which he was famous on the hand ball court. Jenna watched her young husband undress, admiring his athlete's body but as she did a tidal wave of conflicting thoughts and emotions coursed through her. Jenna was a body fitness fanatic and she admired her husband's body almost abstractly like he was a specimen not a human being. But she just could not get over his sexual appetite. His passion rises so fast she thought and he gets so hard.

Look at his penis. It's standing up already and it's so huge. The head is blood red and it's throbbing so dangerously I feel afraid of it. I wish he'd give me some time to get in the mood, wait until the evening. I love him but I can't allow his lust to ruin our marriage. Eddie came to the bed and lay down beside his wife. He reached for her, grasping one full, firm breast in an enormous hand; he massaged it, roughly, the mound of femaleness soft and yielding under his kneading fingers. His great need was apparent in the urgency of his husky voice.

"Jesus, Jenna, I'm so horny. I've got to fuck you now. I want my cock in your cunt." As disgusted as she was by his obscene words and even more lewd demands she tried to remain calm.

"Let's wait until tonight," she pleaded in vain.

Yet she knew he must have heard the growing anger in her voice. Huffing she thought, 'well sure, and just like always he'll ignore my needs and my wants to take care of his own. The selfish bastard!' His hungry lips cut off any further words she might have had, his tongue lashing into her mouth, as his hand left the breast it was massaging and moved downward across her belly, coming to rest on the golden, softly trimmed landing-strip of her pubic mound. His hairy hand was stopped there; he couldn't move it between her thighs and into her pussy because she had clamped her legs tightly together. Jenna twisted her lips away.

"No, Eddie, please let's wait until tonight." Ignoring her feeble entreaties the big man began to insinuate his middle finger into the soft, hair-lined crease, but he couldn't get it in far enough.

"Spread your legs!" he barked out in growing frustration. She obeyed him, reluctantly. Snake-like, he ran his hand down over her pubic hair, cupping the whole of her naked loins in his big hand, pressing it all up tight between her open legs, compressing the folds of flesh, and kneading her, as he had her breast moments before. She gasped and she remembered the furious lovemaking of the previous evening. She did not want to subject herself to his perverted demands again and especially not in the light of the day.

"No... I don't... want it."

"You never do but I have to get my cock inside you. My balls are burning!" Jenna moaned in answer to his frantic demands and the fear in her groin. She wanted him to be satisfied but his demands were just too much for her to put up with any longer. Enough was enough!

"Stop it... you're going to be late for work for your dinner meeting." In answer, his finger went straight to the furrow of her cunt, moving in the pink, tender flesh, insistently digging then moving upward, through the slight moistness to find the hidden bud of her clitoris. He rubbed at it, stroking the tiny button, trying to rouse it to alert erectness, but it lay flaccid and unresponsive under his frantic fingers, refusing to leave its canopied protection. Suddenly, with a desperate gasp, Eddie heaved himself to his knees; he couldn't stand the wait any longer. Kneeling over his wife, he placed himself between her partly spread legs, pushing outward with his muscular thighs to spread her limbs even further apart. Eddie's cock was fully erect, its huge, blood-engorged length jutting out from his torso like another arm. He took the monstrous cock in his hand, and came down, slowly, upon her, as he guided it to the soft, hair-lined slit at the opening of her pussy.

He pressed the lust-inflated head against the reddened flesh of her, trying to force the lust raging cock into her barely moistened and unwilling cunt.

"Stop it, Eddie... I'm not ready... I don't want it."

"You never do. What am I supposed to do with this hard cock of mine?"

"You're an animal... you're unnatural wanting sex all the time like this. You're hurting me," she bleated hoping that even if the statement was untrue it would be enough to cool him down and leave her alone.

Eddie's face froze, the anger rising in him, as he spat out, "so now I'm some kind of beast, am I? Is that what you think about me?"

She was instantly contrite. "No, I didn't really mean it. It just popped out." But Eddie was furious now.

"I want to fuck you within an inch of your life. If you'd get into it, you'd enjoy it." His base, vulgar language was cutting into her like a knife, slicing, slashing and jabbing at her mind. Her body stiffened, and her face froze into a mask of injured self-righteousness.

"I've had enough of this," she said with a voice like ice water thrown in his face, "let me up."

"Oh, Jenna, stop acting like an injured virgin," he said calmly trying to placate her.

"Don't speak to me like that. I won't have it. This is supposed to be lovemaking not that other filthy word you use for it."

"Good Christ, will you be reasonable!" he shot out now completely exasperated.

"You are not being reasonable!" she snapped at him, furiously attempting to release herself from his pinioning embrace. Eddie was rapidly becoming exasperated with her feeble objections and he found that the growing anger within him was dampening his ardor. His cock was still rigid, but the inner turmoil was taking its toll; he could feel the change taking place in him. Some flaccidity of his virile organ was already evident. He tried one more time to get things to a mutually happy solution.

"Come on, Jenna, honey... let's talk about this,"

he began, awkwardly trying to apologize.

"You're not going to treat me like some whore you just picked up off the street," she fumed, twisting herself free of him, finally, and sitting upright on the edge of the bed.

"But, darling, we're married. What do you expect me to do, beat off, all the time?"

"I'm sure I don't care," she said coldly. Rejected yet again he heaved himself up angrily from the bed, gathered up his dirty clothes and plunged toward the bathroom, slamming the door hard behind him.

He turned on the cold shower and jumped under it bathing his aching cock to ease the frustration of his incomplete sexual act. Then, he dressed, quickly, to go back into the city. At least, he could throw himself into work and find some distraction in that but still he well was well aware that he was reaching a breaking point within his own marriage. Love it seemed would not be enough. Maybe it never had been. He seethed, inwardly, his anger mounting higher each moment. Just thinking about the way his new wife constantly thwarted his attentions made pissed him off. Almost everything else in his life was coming together.

He had just been granted some of the really big accounts at the firm; the high dollar ones that would propel him into a partnership if he worked hard enough. It was something he had always wanted to do and this legal firm was top notch all the way. It was really the crème de la crème with all the latest equipment and tech support; anything he needed was there at his beck and call to help create the billable hours. For the first time in his life he felt like he had it made. He had married a gorgeous young virgin who was at the firm one day waiting outside one of the senior partners offices for her grandmother within and it seemed like it was a marriage made in heaven. They made a striking young couple but Eddie thought ruefully, it was all a front. She was like a perfect wedding cake for display in a shop window. Stunning, flawless and looked like everything you could ever want; until you cut into it and found it was made of cardboard scaffold with nothing but hollow dead air inside.

Shit, she doesn't even like me to finger her let alone ever let me eat her cunt. If I could just get her to sample a taste of that she'd probably go out of her mind. God, the first time I did it doggie-style to her instead of missionary, I thought she was going to call the cops. It's my own fault. All the guys said I was an asshole to marry a virgin. I should have found out how she felt about sex before we got married. Now it's too late. It's been almost three months and instead of getting better it's getting worse.

Sitting at the traffic lights, his attention was diverted momentarily; it was the body of a woman that had caught his eye and he was sure that he recognized Sally Dunn in her white tennis dress walking along the street carrying her racquet on the way to the club. That's a body! Jeeeeesus! I've always thought she must be the hottest cunt in the club and every time she saunters by she nearly drives me nuts. I wonder what it would be like inside that hot little cunt? I bet she'd be a fabulous fuck! Eddie, old boy, you're getting a little ahead of yourself. You've gotten married and already you're thinking about other women. This is not a good sign. Christ, though, my cock aches! Why doesn't Jenna let herself go? What makes her so uptight?

Suddenly, he found himself almost abreast of Sally Dunn. The provocative swing of her hips and the flashing smile of recognition she threw over her shoulder toward his new Viper, combined to cause him, on impulse, to steer the car over to the curb and stop beside her. He leaned across the seat, looking up and out at her where she had stopped, waiting, hesitantly.

"Mrs. Dunn... can I give you a ride over to the club?" She trotted over to the low-slung automobile.

"Why Mr. Harris. Hi! You're a lifesaver. I didn't realize it was so far on foot." Eddie opened the car door for her and she got in, revealing her long, tapering legs to good advantage. He smiled then when she glanced over her shoulder to reach for the seat beat he took a good, long look, feasting his eyes on her female loveliness. She had even more beautiful legs than he had remembered from seeing her in the pro shop over at the Marina.

"Where's your car?" he asked her when she had settled herself in the low bucket seat, moving her hands to her hair to fling the long tresses over her shoulders. The movement accented her heaving breasts; the outline of her tits prominent under the thin white material of her tennis dress.

"It stalled just around the corner and I discovered that I had left my wallet at home. I don't have a dime with me and all my credit cards are at home so I'm walking to the club to call David to have the car towed."

"I'm glad I happened along. Always glad to rescue a damsel in distress," he joked, easing the car back into the traffic. Trying to be as unobtrusive as possible, he glanced over at her, appreciatively, noting the swell of her tanned thigh, which the white tennis skirt accentuated. Her legs were bare as far up her thigh as he could see and he wondered about her panties which were the only things keeping her decent. He chuckled silently to himself, not much to stop anyone really he thought. Just flimsy little panties keeping her cunt away from his prying eyes but it was enough that he couldn't stop thinking about what type of undies she might have on.

Against his will, he felt the familiar, pleasurable throb between his legs, as his penis began to engorge with his roaring hot blood, building an erection. His scrotum began to tighten and to pull his testicles up, the crawling sensation, again, making him acutely aware that he had been thwarted in his dinner-time attempt to make love to his own beautiful wife. The need was too much and he took another sidelong look at the lovely olive-skinned beauty of Sally Dunn, her deeply wide-set dark eyes, straight brown hair and her straight attractive nose. Her trim dress fell in natural folds around her breasts, revealing the generous nature of them. The contours, softly rounding, made him wonder whether or not she was wearing a brassiere. The curve of her thigh was firm, her skirt stretching and straining to cover it but slightly.

He followed the curves on down to tapering lower thighs and delicate knees, the calves swelling gently and muscularly. He could see her trim ankles peeping over the tops of her tennis half socks and saw that they were in perfect proportion to the rest of her voluptuous body. Eddie's prick jumped in his boxers. Quickly, he glanced down at himself to ascertain whether his throbbing erection was going to be obvious to his passenger. Sally was a well put together bundle of womanly beauty, he decided, but the fact that she was David Dunn's wife and David was a pro at the club and she worked in the pro shop which made the thought of having any physical contact impossible. She was forbidden by the moral rule that the instructors didn't have anything to do with their clients.

Although he couldn't help but think it was his wife that was the client. Eddie never played tennis. Of course, he couldn't help but notice her around the club and they had exchanged a few brief words but that was it. He wasn't going to let himself be tempted and besides he didn't want to compromise his growing friendship with her husband, David who was a pretty decent guy by all appearances. In this moment, however, he began to see Sally in a new light in view of the events of the last hour with his own wife. She was a fully mature woman... a very desirable woman, and Eddie needed a woman. He stole another glance at her. He decided that she was, definitely a very sexy young woman. I wonder if I should try and come on to her? I wonder if she'd be open to that?

It probably wouldn't be fair to especially thinking about David. After all, I do have to see him on a regular basis. Jesus! I've already got a hard-on. Look at those tits! I'd give my right arm just to feel them. He smiled over at her, noting that her slim, tapering hands were in her lap, the fingers entwined, nervously.

"How's David?" he asked. "Has he had a couple of days off or something? I haven't seen him around for a few days."

"Yes, he took a couple of days off to go to a tournament in Los Angeles."

"Oh, he sure works hard at it, doesn't he?"

"Yeah," She sighed with what sounded like real longing, "I wish he'd work just as hard in other directions," she said smiling wistfully. She turned her head to look out the window. Eddie spoke to the back of her shining head, puzzled by the meaning of her words.

"What's that supposed to mean?"

"It just means that he keeps himself in top condition to play tennis but when it comes to playing with me... well- let's just say, not so much and let it go at that." Her message came over strong and clear, but he was also sure that she, naively, didn't realize the signals she was giving out. She was being only honest, he thought to himself, nothing here- no invitation for a glorious fuck.

His eyes drifted over her, again, liking what he saw more and more, meanwhile his attentions of keeping away from the tennis pro's wife was getting pushed farther and farther into the recesses of his mind by the persistent pulsing of his rock-hard erection between his legs. He decided to probe a little deeper. "Do you mean he's not satisfying you in bed?" he burst out breathlessly.

The dark-haired beauty didn't answer immediately. After a moment, she said. "Yes, that's it." She sighed and dropped her gaze, demurely to her hands, wringing them agitatedly in her lap. Eddie knew just how she felt. There's nothing worse than frustration.

"I'm sorry I said anything," she said suddenly.

"You must think I'm a real bitch."

"No, it's all right. I'm not a marriage counselor just a tax lawyer."

"David doesn't even know I exist, half the time," she sighed ignoring him, turning to look out the window again.

"So that's the problem, he ignores you..." he prompted wanting to get to the bottom of the matter.

"He doesn't want to do it very often. His idea of keeping me happy is to do it a couple of times a month," she said miserably still looking out the window.

"And you want it more often," he queried.

"Well, God. It seems to me to be unnatural to have such a low sex-drive," she said matter-of-factly.

Eddie laughed out loud. A hard bitter laugh which startled and confused her. She jerked her head around to look at him in a wide eyed consternation. "I don't think it's funny."

"Please believe me when I tell you, I know. How well I know! It's amazing. What a rotten coincidence!"

"Coincidence?"

"Yeah... we're in the same boat."

"I don't follow you."

"Jenna is just like David."

"I see." She dropped her gaze again, afraid that she had gone too far in revealing to him an intimate fact of her married life to a comparative stranger. Then Eddie reached out, on impulse, his huge paw settling on her bare knee, gently. The smooth, tanned flesh was warm to his hand, inviting him and tantalizing him with its warm promise. She looked up at him, startled, as his hand massaged the inner part of her knee and began to move upward an inch or so along the soft, smooth flesh of the inside of her thigh.

"Mr. Harris! I hope you don't think that because I told you about David that I'd... I'd..."

She gasped, at a loss for words, her legs clamping together, but the big hand was trapped between her thighs still trying to move upward toward her cunt.

"You're a lovely, desirable woman, Sally, and I want you. I want to make love to you," he rasped out, his breath starting to come in low spurts now.

"Good God! We're both married. How could you even think...?"

"Listen," Eddie cut in, "you just said that David wasn't giving you enough in the sack..."

"Well, yes, but that doesn't mean that I'm going to start hopping in bed with every guy with a boner that comes along." The words came tumbling out of her, as she struggled to find reasons to stop his advances toward her.

"We could be discreet. Keep it on the down-low. No one would ever know," he said.

"You make it sound like going to the supermarket," she said. "I couldn't get involved in something like that. Besides, there are other people to think about."

Overwhelmingly, the burden of his sex was bearing down on him. He felt his prick straining at the confines of his shorts. It was standing up, painfully, throbbing, alert; demanding his attention. Christ! How this woman had aroused him. He wanted her, but he knew that it was impossible. Silently, they rode along for a few moments, then Eddie, again, reached out his hand to her thigh. She shifted in the bucket seat, and almost imperceptibly her legs spread for his hand as it gained the inside of her thigh and moved upward along the warm flesh to the heat of her crotch. Quickly, he made his decision. She was ready!

"You're dying for it, aren't you?" he said, making his question a statement of fact.

"No. You're wrong. I can't do it. It wouldn't be right." Her thighs closed on his hand, and he felt a slight thrust of her hips; a gentle uncontrolled, grinding motion that made her words a lie, her body speaking the truth of her need.

"Where can we go? Obviously, we can't go to your place or my place."

"Mmm," she gasped, her hips straining forward even more. He frowned, time was of the essence. His hand was at the juncture of her thighs. He used his fingers, probing until he found the crease below the pubic mound and insinuated his middle finger. He pushed against her and found the bud of her womanhood under the thin wisp of nylon.

"No... Please... I can't stand it... no," she gasped with pleasure. Her words jolted him. Now, he was beginning to have second thoughts about the whole thing. He began to wonder if he might have gotten himself in too deeply, already, as he thought about the bizarre situation. They were both aroused sexually and there seemed to be no immediate answer to where they could go and fuck.

"Let's go to a motel," he suggested.

"It would take too long to get there," she murmured, her eyes glazed and passion-filled.

"All right, I know what we'll do," he said. "There's equipment hut behind the pro shop..."

"Isn't that kind of risky...?"

"You're right. We'll park behind it and just stay in

the car. We'll manage. Where there's a will there's a way." Pulling his fingers from her cunt, he turned into the drive of the tree-shaded club and threaded his way around the member's parking lot around to the rear of the pro shop to the employee's lot. No one else seemed to be around and he parked the car over to the corner of the small lot, quickly turning off the ignition and reaching for her. Eagerly, readily, Sally came into his arms, lifting her lips to him willingly, and moving as close to him as the bucket seats of the expensive Viper would allow.

Their lips met, and her tongue came probing into his mouth, wetly, seeking him. He was pleasantly surprised by her wanton search of his oral cavity, her lingual member hotly slithering into all its crevices. He sensed the urgency in the woman and thrust his own tongue forward to joust, momentarily with hers, before giving her just the tip of it. She instantly, voraciously, sucked on his tongue, pulling it deeply into her warm, hungry mouth. At the same time his hands were occupied with her body. He found her breasts, to his delight, they were completely unfettered. She wore no bra under her tennis dress. The swell of her thigh was firm and long tapering and he reveled in the wonderful womanliness of her. His strong hands explored all her curves, massaging her, roughly, molding and kneading her, and her breath came fast into his mouth. Frustrated, he broke the kiss.

"We're not going to be able to do anything in this car. It's just too small." Shyly, she smiled up at him, her face framed by her long, dark-brown hair, not knowing how to say the thing she wanted to say, yet knowing that it must be stated, somehow, if they were to finish what they had unknowingly started.

"We could take turns," she said, her voices scarcely louder than a murmur, "take turns doing it to each other." It was at that moment that she saw it. Her dark eyes drank in the throbbing bulge at his crotch revealing his desire for her. She reached out to him, her tiny hand trembling slightly as she rested it, momentarily on his bare knee, then dragged her fingers with a slithering motion up the inside of his thigh, feather-touching his hardened prick. As she withdrew her hand his cock jerked up hard, and he could feel the moistness at the tip of it. She smiled up into his eyes, laying her hand gently on his huge bicep, she squeezed, meaningfully and finished.

"Do you know what I mean?"

"I get the picture," he said, "are you sure?"

"Well, it's the only thing we can do here in this little space," she said blushing thinking she had already been too bold.

"You don't have to do it, Sally," he started to say surprised that she would initiate such a thing. His own wife Jenna would never in a million years entertain such an idea.

"I want to. We can do it right now." "We could go out tonight and find somewhere," he suggested hopefully. She reflected for a moment.

"I don't know. David will be home. But maybe we could come back here."

"Super," he said. "The courts close at ten, I've got a key. I'll meet you back here." The more he thought about it, the more he realized that the lounge of the fitness club would be the perfect place. He wondered that he had not thought of it before this. He gave a wicked grin and realized being a chartered member with a key finally had been worth the ridiculous price of admission. Again, he took her in his muscular tanned arms and kissed her with passionate abandon. She stopped him momentarily, her dark eyes smoky and lust glazed, as she lifted her hips, raised her tennis dress high and reaching down, slid her panties down over her swelling thighs, exposing the olive-toned nakedness of her buttocks to him; then she slid down into the seat moving her pelvis up and forward.

Unerringly, Eddie's big hand went down between her legs to her pubic mound, the black, curling hair tingling in his palm. As his finger found the erect bud of her clitoris, she moaned with sensual pleasure, her hips beginning to rotate sensuously and snake-like up against his hand. He put his arm behind her and levered her forward while he unzipped the back of her white tennis dress. Inserting his arm inside the dress, he put his arm around her and captured a full naked breast in his hand. She leaned back against him as he began to massage the smooth flesh mounding under his fingers grasping the nipple between thumb and forefinger, he urged it to stiff erectness.

"God," she murmured, "your hands are doing wonderful things to my body."

"Ohhhh, baby..." he mumbled. Now, the moistness of her furrow told him she was stimulated, ready, and he inserted two fingers in her cunt, moving them in slowly, spreading her to receive them, and feeling the soft resiliency of the inner lining of her vaginal walls. He leaned over and kissed her, thrusting his tongue into her throat, stiffly.

She took it, sucked it deeply into her mouth, making tiny mewling sounds in her throat. Abruptly, she broke away from him, looking up into his face with half-closed, glazing eyes. She reached out to him, placing her hand behind his heavily muscled neck and gently drew his head downward to her loins. Her silent but eloquent message sent a thrill through him, spearing into his loins and making his cock pulsate, jarringly, inside his pants.

He was aware of a good deal of moisture on the head of his prick and that it was soaking through the cloth of his trousers. He removed his arm from around her, inside her tennis dress, and she leaned farther back into the corner of the seat, spreading her legs widely for him, as his great head was lowered to her soft, darkly, hair-lined pussy. His tongue slid out to her, touching her pulsating clitoris, the damp warmth of the quivering erect mystery of her driving him on. He made circles with his tongue, feeling it grow even more erect, pulsing under his lips. Then, more maddeningly for her, he began stroking up and down on the short length of her clitoral bud, as her hips ground in circles thrusting up into his face with urgent demands. The pungent taste of her spurred him onward. He took the bud in his lips, drawing the erectile tissue into his mouth to suck upon it. Then, he bared his teeth and gave the tiny nipple of her cunt a gentle little nip. Sally almost exploded under him, as she groaned out her pleasure.

"My God... ooooh!" he heard her moan as his tongue moved on her like lightning, igniting lascivious fires of passion deep within her hungering loins. Eddie strained forward in the confines of the car, reaching out with his tongue to probe into the narrow slit of her pussy. His tongue went into her, and he began to move it in and out, flicking it from his mouth to the rhythm she had already set in her wildly gyrating pelvis. Sally began to move faster. He went back to her clitoris and licked her, furiously, as she arched up at him off the seat of the Viper grinding her open cunt with wild abandon into his face. Moving up and down her furrow, she felt his tongue, alive on her, lashing at her clitoris, accelerating her on, moving her upward, where she soared with ecstasy of her passion to the heights, and there was a great rushing, whistling wind in her ears, as great, explosive spasms of orgasmic relief wracked her body. She gasped and moaned out her delight, wanting him to go on and on.

"Eddie... my God... faster... keep on harder... oh eat me... I'm.... going to...ooooh... I'm there... I'm gonna come." The small brunette's body arched off the seat in a final spasm of climax and collapsed in final release as wave after wave of relaxing euphoria overcame her.

"Aaaah... oooooh... thank you... it was... wonderful!" she said, as she ran her fingers languidly through his short bristly hair. She closed her eyes and leaned back in the bucket seat of the tiny foreign car savoring the warmth of her sensations. Eddie's head was in her lap, her naked thighs and buttocks exposed, and he gently rubbed his hand along the silky smoothness of her, waiting for her, allowing her to luxuriate for a few moments... until she would be ready to manipulate him to sexual release. Finally, she stirred after a few moments, and Eddie raised himself to a sitting position. Her delicate hand reached out to his zippered fly. He heard the metallic whisper of it as she opened his trousers, dipped in a cool hand and liberated his throbbing penis, bringing it out into the car with them.

Sally Dunn leaned over him, slithering her body around in the seat until her head was directly over his cock. With one hand she grasped the shaft of it, her hand barely able to wrap completely around its circumference. Slowly, she pulled the foreskin back to reveal the purplish red cowl of the glans from which a trickle of the viscous preparatory juices ran. She scratched her fingernails lightly over the length of it, as the great rod strained upward, pointing at her, and Eddie could feel the hot moistness of her breath flowing over the smooth rubbery head. Jenna! Suddenly his wife's name popped into his over-stimulated brain.

Jesus Christ! What am I doing? I've only been married a couple of months and already I'm picking up other women. I have no right to do this kind of thing even if Jenna did put me off... I must be flipping my cookies to be eating some woman's cunt in broad daylight out here behind the tennis club. If Clay Marsdale or any of the other directors caught me it could mean my membership! The guilt stricken husband swallowed deeply; his decision was actually made for him. He was too far along, and there was no stopping, now. He trembled with an emotion he had never before experienced. This was new to him, even though he knew what was coming, he didn't know what to expect from it, until he felt her lips encircle the entire head of his cock, absorbing it into the warm, wet confines of her mouth. The keening sensation knifed through him, his whole body vibrating with the lewd sensuality of it. Her warm, moist mouth on the sensitive, pulsing head of his prick was like nothing he had ever imagined. Then he thought he would die!

She began to suck on his cock with tantalizingly rhythmic movements, her tongue moving in swirls around the head of it while her head began a slow up and down bobbing with a slight twist on each up stroke. Eddie looked down to watch her, and the sensations she was producing in him were trebled as he saw how much of his hard fleshy rod of dangerous aroused meat she was taking into her delicately modeled mouth. She was moaning softly and taking almost his entire massive cudgel into her oral cavity, as her head bobbed sensuously up and down over his hairy loins. He began to move his hips in instinctive opposition to her and was further amazed when all of his lust-hardened cock seemed to disappear into her soft bruised lips. Now, using her teeth, she began to suck harder allowing them to scrape along the length of his hardened flesh, leaving white marks in the skin where she bit into it with gentle nips. Her tongue was alive and busy in her mouth; its nerve-tingling lick on the outstroke was making the head of his member throb and jerk, signaling him of his rising passion.

It felt like an urge to relieve himself but the damming action of the tumescent flesh held the seminal flow in check until it would be time. He could feel the beginnings of it deep in his loins, his testicles drawn up below ready to discharge their waiting load of semen. Tenderly, reaching out a hand to her, he tangled his fingers in her hair, feeling that he should help her to set the pace. He watched, fascinated, as he saw the flesh of her lips being pulled in and out, and he marveled at her technique, her sexual knowledge, knowing instinctively that she had performed this sex act before, probably with her own husband David

Dunn. Beginning to get more desperate now, he began to move more rapidly, jerking his hips up into her face, ramming his member without mercy into her mouth, as he felt the surge within him and his cock seemed to grow even larger in her mouth. She kept pace with him, never missing a beat. Eddie knew he was near the zenith now. He could feel the dammed up pressure of it beginning to reach the point of no return and suddenly the walls of the dam were down!

Breathlessly, he gasped, "Sally... sweet Jesus, baby... I'm nearly there..." The spewing semen came in a rush, jetting into her mouth in great spurts of viscous, white jets of thickly hot fluid. She swallowed and kept swallowing, as wave after wave of it was sucked from him.

"Shit! Oh Jesus! I'm coming! Don't stop... don't stop sucking my cock!" he gasped out at her, ramming her head down farther onto his jerking prick, his hips bucking up at her wildly. Happily she went on sucking, her lips hollowing in and out, as he continued spewing his load into her mouth, his rod plunging up at her, mercilessly, its entire length buried in her throat. He felt as though he had been turned inside out, the drawing sensations seeming to start in his bowels. Then, as his prick continued with smaller and smaller pumping spasms, she went on, gently, nibbling and licking the last drops of the white liquid sperm from his moisture glistening cock. Eddie groaned out his satisfaction leaning back into the car seat, his eyes closed, as he savored the effects of his orgasm.

Gradually, his member began to deflate in her mouth, its tumescence beginning to make it flaccid and limber, again. So lost in their lewd activities were the two adulterous companions that they did not notice the hasty retreat of a man in tennis whites slinking back towards the door of the building. The man had been taking the video tape equipment back to the court where he taped the progress of the players and then played it back for them so that they could instantly review their errors. He hadn't expected this unexpected bonus. His digital recorder had been able to zero in on the erotic scene. Sally Dunn released his slowly deflating prick, allowing it to pull from her mouth, as she rolled her head to one side of his knees. She continued to look at it in fascination, almost hypnotized by the deflating action. Finally, she looked up at Eddie, emitting a sigh and raising her lips to him for a kiss. Eddie took her in his arms and kissed her full on the mouth, inserting his tongue to taste the essence of his own cum still remaining somewhat pungent in her mouth. It was she that broke the kiss.

"Did you like me sucking your cock?"

"Oh, baby... fucking awesome... out of this world!" "Just wait until later," she promised. "Wait... my balls will be in a knot all day, Mrs. Sally Dunn!"

CHAPTER 2

Jenna's smooth, long-legged tanned beauty topped by her upswept golden sun-streaked hair was reflected back to her in the bathroom mirror as she stepped gingerly from the tiled shower on to the fluffy bath mat. Vigorously, she toweled herself dry, being especially careful of the up-thrusting mounds of her breasts; they were rather tender to the touch and in particular the darker pink of the nipples, standing erect now from the stimulation of the terry toweling. She looked into the mirror with intense inspection. The young blonde wife surveyed her body minutely as she catalogued the areas where she could still feel the imprint of Eddie's strong hands. She examined the creamy, lustrous skin of the generous hemispheres of both breasts. She felt almost disappointed that there were no marks because they would have been proof to her what an absolute sexual beast her husband was and how selfish and unfeeling he was towards her.

Running her hands over her body, she winced with disgust as she became aware of tender places on her curving thighs and rounded buttocks. Then, her hands found the silky triangle of her womanhood, moving, gently, over the private parts of her, there exploring any damage he might have done. With both hands now, she spread the lips to determine the extent of the havoc her lust-maddened husband had played upon her genitals during his desperate attempt at a "quickie". She ran a finger, cautiously, into the slit and around the vaginal opening; the raw, exposed nerve endings signaled, their tender state. She moved onward, upward to the clitoral bud, instantly feeling the electric tingle of sensual pleasure as she touched it. She did not dwell there. The thought the very idea that she might generate in herself a towering, sexual climax ran counter to every fiber of her conscious being. High class ladies her mother had always counseled her did not ever dare abuse themselves with liquor, drugs or sex. Every time I've felt like doing it to myself, there it is. It's in my brain yelling loudly. It's a sin in the eyes of God. Don't do it. Maybe that's the reason I can't be the kind of woman Eddie wants me to be. I even try to stop him from touching me there. But, Lord, how I've desired him to do it anyway.

Even in the privacy of her own bathroom, she felt the flush spreading in her cheeks as the thought of the pleasure she had received, on those few times, when Eddie had stroked her clitoris to hard erectness, bringing her a feeling of indecent shame. Jenna was trying desperately to rationalize her conditioning. Life in Salt Lake City with her strict Mormon upbringing gave the young woman little chance to think for herself. The strict religious community of which her family played a leading role gave her little chance to do anything without the watchdog eyes of everyone upon her. Always present and in the forefront was the consideration of what other people thought... about what you did, or didn't do. Her church life had been her entire life and even though she did not have a religious nature naturally her conditioning had imposed one on her. And now even though she was almost two thousand miles away from Salt Lake City she still felt like the eyes of the Elders of the church were on her. Judging her. Judging -always judging and Jenna ever in fear of being found wanting. Just not good enough; always found wanting with her parents bowing their heads knowing their daughter was not doing her duty.

Her body had escaped the physical restraints of the place, but her mind was still bound, an unwilling prisoner of her past. She dressed quickly, covering her body, blotting out its demanding sensuality from herself. In the face of the growing awareness of her need... a desire for sexual fulfillment, she could not trust herself; her beautiful young body reflected in the mirror screamed for it, and she was frightened. The naughty part of her mind knew that she only had to reach her hand out to herself to gain a pleasurable release but her reasoning conditioned mind rejected it, completely. She glanced at the clock as she finished dressing, noticing that it was almost six o'clock. Already and she had so much to do.

Oh God, she thought. I was supposed to go over to Nina Marsdale's for drinks this evening. This was the day she'd been invited by Mrs. Marsdale, wife of the director of the Marina Tennis Clinic to socialize with some of the other women associated with the club and she was rather pleased about it. She was slowly being accepted into this 'waspish' enclave of wealthy old money who had looked at her out of the corners of their eyes when she had first arrived. Quickly, she dabbed some perfume behind her ears and frantically raced around looking for her car keys. At last she found them and was on her way.

She arrived a little late but hoped that Mrs. Marsdale was sufficiently flexible to tolerate tardiness. Nina Marsdale stood framed in the doorway in answer to the doorbell, a radiant smile on her lips, her beautiful, Oriental eyes accented, tastefully, dominated her doll-like face. The Chinese woman was much shorter than Jenna, perfectly proportioned and she stood with the animal grace of the exotic dancer she was before marrying Clay Marsdale. She moved toward Jenna to an inner rhythm of her own, her body under complete control, projecting an image of the completely realized woman, fulfilled, self-confident and madly in love with life. She spoke with a warm, throaty, softly modulated voice, her slight Oriental accent charming but her English was cultured and correct.

"Oh Jenna, you look lovely today. You really have a great tan... come in."

"Thank you, Nina," Jenna said following her in. Nina steered her expertly among the women gathered in small groups, introducing her graciously to those whom she did not know; finally leaving her over at the bar where a bartender was taking drink orders. The chatter and gossip of the women was really juicy and she was soon caught up in it, listening to them, as they wittily ripped to shreds all their friends who were not there. Feeling too new to the group, and also not knowing many of the people, Jenna contented herself with only a few nods or interjections. Gradually, the women began to filter out of the Marsdale's residence back to their homes as it was nearing the dinner hour.

"Why don't you stay and have another drink?" Nina invited. Although liquor had been a strict taboo in the Mormon religion Jenna had rather turned her back on the church now to some extent and did have a social drink now and again more out of politeness than any great desire for its effects. As a 'Jack Mormon' her family had hopes she had not fully abandoned her religious codes but Jenna was pulling further away every year since college. After all it was her grandmother's idea for her to go to school out here and Jenna had decided never to go back once she tasted life on the coast.

"Yes, all right, but only a small one," Jenna accepted. Nina poured from a chilled pitcher, the clear liquid cascading into the stemmed glasses with a refreshing fragrance. Jenna knew that she was able to cope very well on one martini but against her better judgment and Nina's insistent urging finally breaking her resistance, she accepted a second. Jenna found that the Mrs. Marsdale was a wonderful listener, as the alcohol loosened her inhibited feeling and she began to pour out her soul to the older woman. Nina listened with sympathy while Jenna told of her fears and frustrations concerning her sex life with Eddie since their recent wedding.

"My poor, poor, darling," Nina said with some animation. "You haven't yet learned that sex isn't a one-way street. You are every bit as entitled to fulfillment from it as Eddie. You have to make your demands known to your husband or otherwise he can't know what turns you on. You'll want to indulge yourself magically in anything that will bring you to full orgasm." The Oriental woman's eyes were shining bright and excited and she warmed to her topic.

Jenna made objections, saying, "But, Nina, some of the things he wants me to do are filthy, perverted, and unnatural. I'm perfectly willing to do the regular stuff, but this other stuff is just too much for me to handle."

"Jenna! Good Lord! I'm really astonished that you don't know that these things are a part of most married couple's life. Believe me, there's nothing wrong with them, as long as you both end up having a genuine sexual experience. Clay and I constantly experiment with new things just to find ways of equally fulfilling each other."

The conversation went on longer than Jenna had anticipated. Nina got very graphic explaining, naming and describing in detail various positions and techniques for erotic gratification and she felt her cheeks flame as the list grew. It seemed to her that each new category was more depraved than the last; until, finally, her mind was in a whirl, not only from the effects of the alcohol, but also, from the sheer effort of trying to understand Nina's dissertation and her liberal attitudes toward them. Finally, in desperate embarrassment, Jenna pleaded a headache and the lateness of the hour, reminding Mrs. Marsdale that she would have to go home as Eddie would soon be there worrying if she was not. Nina had finished her third martini on top of what she had consumed before but Jenna had had the good sense to limit herself to two of the potent drinks.

As it was, tiny Mrs. Marsdale was beginning to slur her words, and her genteel vocabulary became salted with more than a few lewd references. Gradually, Jenna began to see another side of Nina Marsdale. It was the shocking realization that the woman underneath the sophisticated veneer was somewhat lewd, salacious, sometimes vulgar, but not, she conceded, coarse. Vaguely, she began to wonder what the other woman's background might be, and how it was that she was married to the fabulously wealthy Clay Marsdale. It would be very interesting to know these things, she thought. She had heard rumors that Nina had been a 'dancer' but of course that was never spoken aloud within Nina's hearing. Yet Jenna couldn't help but wonder if it was true and that was why Nina was so comfortable with sex. Holding the door for Jenna as she left, Nina's face was flushed slightly and her speech was growing sloppy. She extended an invitation to Jenna but this one included her husband, Eddie.

"We'll have to get that handsome husband of yours off the hand-ball courts and have you and him over some night. We'll play some new games. I get so tired of tennis, tennis, tennis. Clay lives, eats and sleeps tennis with very few digressions. At least your Eddie plays something different."

"That would be nice, Nina," Jenna assured her. "Just name the day. I'm sure Eddie would be pleased to accept, too."

"Perhaps we can play a little game of charades demonstrating the ways of sex, huh?" Jenna didn't reply, she didn't have to-her face and neck were scarlet with embarrassment. She walked out to her car feeling more than a little bit confused, her head in a whirl and a welter of conflicting thoughts rushing madly, through her mind.

'Did I understand correctly what Nina meant by that last remark? I find it hard to believe that Nina would say those things? Why they're terribly lewd. I don't usually even think about such things. All that disgusting stuff that Eddie's always after me to do to him or that he wants to do to me. I don't care what anyone says. They're sinful and perverted. But Nina says that most people do those things and really enjoy them. And, she even seemed to be hinting that I could enjoy them too. It's just all too confusing for me. What does it have to be so filthy?' Eddie was already preparing a late drink when Jenna came in. She tried to bring up the dinner-time fiasco thinking that if they talked about it, it wouldn't be such a huge problem. But, to her complete amazement, instead of being furious, he just brushed it aside with an apparent lack of concern.

"It's no big deal, Jenna. We'll get it together, yet," he told her, hardly looking at her. In fact his lack of concern felt like outright dismissal. If anything it appeared he couldn't have cared one way or the other if she just walked out of the room leaving him alone for the rest of the night.   She began to look forward to their evening together, vowing to herself that she would try to be more responsive in bed with Eddie. Nina's little talk this afternoon had had some effect after all and she was really secretly hoping that she would have a second chance to prove that she was a sexually exciting woman. Maybe, she'd even consent tonight to trying out one of those wildly unnatural positions that her new friend had described to her in detail. For some reason, though, tonight, Eddie seemed very distracted and she couldn't figure out why since he'd said that he wasn't annoyed about the near argument they had had earlier. What could it be? Had he grown weary of her to the point of not caring already? The newlywed was hoping that her opportunity for a truly fulfilling night with her husband would come to pass this very evening. But, her hopes were short-lived, when after reading some Law News magazine and quickly flipping through the regular newspaper, he announced that he was meeting two new clients and was probably going out later with them for a drink. Eddie called over his shoulder as he left the house, "don't wait up for me, Jenna, sometimes I get so involved I forget the time."

CHAPTER 3

Clay Marsdale arrived home after just having beaten the pants off one of his new pros. The competitive older man was ecstatic when he could still slaughter a much younger man on the courts. He'd done everything else now in life and after retiring early tennis had become his passion. He parked his Mercedes in the large garage and went directly to his screening room. Clay was a gadget fanatic and his newest craze was having all matter of video equipment. He especially loved the Go-Pro which he could attach onto his ball cap and make mini-documentaries with both on the court and at home with his amazing little sex fiend of a wife. He had a screening room that he bragged to neighbors was for the latest movies out on Blue-Ray but in reality he usually watched home-made tidbits. Anxiously, he took the memory card out and put it in the machine and with a couple of adjustments the image slowly materialized on the giant screen. There was a knock on the door. "Clay, darling, are you here?" Nina asked softly. "Yes, baby, hang on for a second." The figures were clearly visible and identifiable on the screen. He hit pause and gave himself a happy giggle then strolled over to the door.

"Come my darling, have I got something sweet to show to you," he laughed with pleasure. Nina was carrying a shaker of martinis and two glasses. Clay gratefully accepted one from her and kissed his wife full on the lips. He could smell the alcohol on her breath and he knew that she had quite a head-start on him. "Just what the doctor ordered," he said looking over her trim figure. She was clad in a pair of French cut beige gabardine pants and a pure silk beige silk shirt tied under her breasts and left unbuttoned sufficiently to reveal the cleavage fully exposed and the upper surfaces of her newly paid for breasts swelling out provocatively. There was no underwear line visible under the blouse or the slacks. He sipped appreciatively at the martini, as he gazed at his exotic wife, a slightly suggestive leer beginning to form around his mouth.

"Dry enough for you, darling?" she asked.

"Terrific, just like you."

He reached out a hand to her and cupped a breast in his strong fingers. It was as he had hoped. She was not wearing a bra under her shirt. He felt the beginnings of arousal and wondered why on earth he had waited so long to buy her new tits. She looked amazing!

"Did you miss your little wife, Clay?"

She pulled away from him and modeled the outfit she was wearing, striking an obscene pose at the end of the demonstration; her hips pulled forward, her arms back, causing her breasts to strain for release from her blouse. Then she undulated her hips, sensually, suggestively, performing a sexually exciting dance just for him. "Did I...? Christ, do you want me to fuck you right here in the screening room?" His eyes were glazing over with lust.

"Actually I prefer the bearskin in the living room... but I'm not particular, darling," she teased. Nina took a sip from her martini and suddenly she noticed that there was something on the screen.

"Well, Fellini, what do we have here?" she asked him.

"Oh, these are my new stars," he said. "You know how I like my little cinema verite."

Nina laughed and walked closer to the giant screen. "Why, Clay this is really exceptional. Who's the woman?"

"She's working part-time in the pro shop. She's David Dunn's wife. Her name's Sally. Sweet little Sally."

"Sally the sweet little cocksucker," Nina corrected and just look at that hunk of meat she's got in her mouth.

Then Nina choked out a laugh as the camera panned up and she got a glimpse of the face behind the steering wheel.

"Oh my, my, what have we here? Isn't that Eddie Harris she's sucking off?" she asked a salacious grin curling around the corners of her lips. "That's him. The whole package." Nina continued watching the action on the screen. "Baby, he is hung, to say the least."

Clay Marsdale looked at his wife, shrewdly. "You like that piece of meat, huh, baby?"

"And how. I'm getting wet just looking at it," the Oriental woman said lewdly. "I thought you would," he said very sure of himself.

"How'd you like to sample it?"

"No samples. I want the full meal!" she exclaimed. "All right, my darling, he's all yours. I'm going to have them over Saturday night for cocktails." Nina was not at all surprised he would try.

"Them?" she asked. "You're not going to invite them? Both of them? I mean really darling his wife is lovely but it would take dynamite to get the stick out of her ass she's so uptight."

"Of course, them. It's a package deal, darling. I don't want one without the other."

"You don't know her too well, do you?" Nina asked her voice pointedly sarcastic.

"What's that supposed to mean?"

"We had a little talk this afternoon and apparently little Ms. Mary Mormon thinks fucking is disgusting or against nature or something. She's really a Goddamn little prude. Getting her to swap even a soft swap, Clay, is going to be a major undertaking."

"I dare say I can warm her up a little. I probably have a lot more experience than that stud husband of hers."

"I'm sure you can, dear," Nina said distractedly. "I'm going to make another shaker of martinis and then I want to see what a stud I'm married to. Don't go away, lover."

Nina left the screening room swishing her hips at him, provocatively. He gave her a playful slap on the ass, grabbing at the firm flesh for good measure.

"Oh, does my little wife, want to indulge in unnatural behavior this evening?"

"Bet your ass, I do," she said closing the door. Clay waited a few minutes and when Nina didn't return he knew that she was probably playing one of her little games where she wanted him to go in search of her. The happy husband chuckled to himself; he was one lucky bastard and he damn well knew it. This is what kept life interesting, exciting and adventurous. He never knew where Nina would choose to have their little sexual bouts.

Clay had had hundreds of women in his lifetime but had always become bored after a while with each but with Nina there was no possibility of boredom. It was almost as if the tiny woman had been schooled in the ways of delighting a man and indeed she had in her native Taiwan but she only hinted at; for all he knew she was making all that shit up to tease him. Either it worked. He couldn't' get enough of her even after ten years. Clay eagerly began walking from room to room in the well-equipped mansion. At last, he heard music in the large room where they usually entertained. The room was done in Italian provincial and as he entered he saw the lights had been dimmed and at first he didn't see his small wife. Usually they chose to hear classical music in this room because it seemed to go with the mood and decoration of the room but tonight Nina had put on a grinding dance record and when he caught sight of her his heart began to beat harder. In the middle of the room was an imported Italian marble fountain around which were placed statues caned by a master carver from Florence.

The statues were in the style of the "David" and all the genitals were executed to scale. Nina was entwined with the white marble statue and she was doing a quick bumping dance, rubbing her female loins, obscenely, against the cold lifelike genitals of the statue.

"So, you're two-timing me, again!" he said jovially.

"The martini shaker is on the table. Pour them will you darling?" she asked her voice low and throaty. He went over and poured the fresh drinks, taking a seat to watch his wife's lewd entertainment. From experience she knew that she had his full attention now and suddenly she leaped on top of their heavy glass coffee table where she threw herself with abandon into a wild lewdly exciting dance, her hips moving in circles and the muscles of her belly rippling and undulating in time to the driving bass driven beat. Marsdale watched his tiny Oriental wife with fascination. She was a superb dancer and he marveled at her muscular control, the sensuousness of her movements and her projected sexuality that never failed to arouse him. She had kept up with her dancing even after their marriage.

He felt the familiar crawling, tensing sensation in his scrotum and the rush of throbbing hot blood into his penis, as it began to rise to erection under his tennis gear that he had not changed yet since his arrival home. He wanted to rip off his sports clothes, grab her and lay her on the glass coffee table, but he had found long ago that it was better to play her game. When she was ready she would let him know. He must wait for her, and he had learned to wait, to reap the benefits of the waiting in heightened enjoyment for both of them. She ended her dance and Nina Marsdale slid lithely from the glass topped table, casting about an eye for her drink. And then she came to him. Insinuating her narrow hips between his legs, she put her arms around his neck and kissed him, long, hard and deep, using her tongue to probe and titillate.

After some moments, she broke the hiss and trailed her tongue across his jowls to his ear. Her tongue lashed out, the tip of it drilling into his ear and running in little circles around it.

She whispered, "My darling, Clay."

The older man set his drink down on the bar and reached for her, grabbing a churning buttock in each hand, he pulled, roughly, to his hardening prick, letting her feel the warmth and stiffness of him.

"Jesus Christ! Nina, you're hotter than a firecracker tonight. I can't wait!" Nina twisted from his grasp and twirled across the floor to a new song from the stereo; then, as she came back to the glass table, she continued her dance for a few moments, before sinking slowly to her knees; finally, she lay prone, posing prettily, upon the glass table top with the inlaid Italian mirrors around it.

"Pass me my drink, Clay, darling, I'm starting to fade." He handed her the martini. She sipped from it, her lovely slanted eyes smoldering, smokily, at him over the brim of the small glass. She smiled an inscrutable little smile at him.

"What are you waiting for husband, dear?" With a little smile she rolled to her stomach on the mirrored table, sipping again from her martini. Clay drained his glass and set it down on the bar. He came off his seat and he came to her running a hand along the smooth contours of her back and bottom. His cock was rock hard, throbbing, alert and ready and he tried to slip his hand under the waistband of her slacks.

"Not so fast, big boy," she said teasingly, as she rolled over onto her back. Clay leaned over her and kissed her hard with his lips and tongue, thrusting deeply into her mouth, sucking the sweet nectar of her. His hands were busy with the buttons of her silk blouse, and the magnificent mounds of firm, full flesh came bursting from their confinement, proudly peaked when he had unbuttoned the last button. Quickly, he glued his mouth to one nipple, sucking and nipping it to erection, causing her to moan in throaty pleasure, as he massaged the other breast with his hand, kneading the silky, smoothness of them and teasing the pink-hued nipple between his thumb and finger. At this point, his hand left her breast, and went in search of other things, down across her belly, smoothing down the swell of her gently rounded hip and back to the inside of her thigh to the soft, inner juncture, where he allowed his hand to roam around the fleecy softness of her gently squirming pubic mound. Then, his hand dipped between her thighs, as she parted them for him, allowing him full access to the tight, elastic nether ring of her cunt.

He insinuated his middle finger into the crease, forcing the cloth of her pants into the moist, vaginal opening. Clay broke the kiss, went around to the end of the table, grabbed his wife by the ankles and heaved her toward him until her buttocks were even with the mirrors of the table. He pulled at her zipper and gave her slacks a hard yank down over her hips, smoothly, suddenly, exposing her warm, slightly throbbing cunt to him, its darkly hair-lined slit staring up at him with moist, viscous droplets of libidinous liquid glistening along the furrow. Marsdale's head came down, and he clamped his lips to her cunt, his tongue coming out to find the warm lips of her womanhood, as Nina moaned in ecstatic pleasure above him. He probed into the dark recesses of her, tasting the pungency aroma, and the moisture of his mouth mingled with the love droplets she emitted there.

The sensations he generated in her loins raced through her like heat lightning. His tongue seared her with its snake-like searching's, and she moved her pelvis upward to his face, draping her legs over his shoulders to afford her more comfort and her husband easier access to the searing seat of her passion. Clay licked and sucked, his tongue lashing up and down the slit, making plunging forays into the moist channel; finally, discovering the clitoris rising from its soft, hair-lined slit, erupting into hardened erection, pulsating warmly as his tongue circled it, tantalizing it, urging it on to even greater sensation producing, nerve-tingling sexuality. She reached for his head, grasping the short, bristly scruff and pulled him in closer to her moving her hips in circles under his insistent mouth and tongue, opening her thighs to him, wantonly, invitingly, urging him on to greater enhancement and the more inventive manipulations of his tongue in her cunt.

Clay looked at his beauty, his gem of a wife and had just begun to think that he could wait no longer to bury his throbbing cock in her, when he felt her move under him, trying to sit up, as she pushed his head away from her. She hissed at him, the words coming as naturally to her as the act itself.

"Come on Clay. Fuck me now. Shove your fat cock in my cunt and make me scream! Now!" In a moment he had flung off his tennis whites as she reached down to him, taking his huge cock in her hands, retracting the foreskin smoothly and guiding the red, hooked knob of it to the cunt lips below, and he came into her with a rush, the head entering her vaginal hole with a wetly sliding action, the thick shaft being absorbed entirely, as he thrust up into her with an animal-like lunge.

"Baby... baby!" she groaned as his great cannon was buried in her soft femaleness, the hardness of it ramming into her, deeply to the very core of her existence. The moist jungle heat of her captured him, enveloped him, as he went into her, the exquisite folds of her cunt clamping around him and he could feel the inner muscles of her vagina caressing his prick, milking it, the sensations torturing him, as he held the length of it in her, not moving yet and his whole being was there in his cock, inside her soft, smooth-walled passage. Clay began to fuck into her with short, quick thrusts, upward into her pussy, standing there, between her legs, using the strength of his back and powerful legs to ram his huge member home into her tender and softly clasping cunt.

"Harder! Clay, do it faster, harder, deeper. Fuck me and make me feel it!" she gasped out to him. His huge, blood-engorged member began to drive deeper and longer into her, its breadth pulling the soft, ragged edge of her furrow out with it on each outstroke, revealing the moist, pink lining of her pussy; then, on the plunging in-stroke, all of it was rammed back into her again. Nina could feel the giant staff of him rampaging into her generating her desire, and she could not get enough of him, as she incessantly urged him on with groans of pleasure, interspersed with her specific groaned out demands. Sometimes she chanted in rhythm of their thrashing bodies, her pelvis moving in opposition to him, wildly, in uncontrolled passion.

"Fuck me. Fuck me. Fuck me. Harder. Harder," she screamed in a frantic need to be stuffed to the hilt with his cock. Marsdale ground into his tiny wife, flexing his knees to gain more leverage and strength, as her buttocks squirmed uncontrollably on the glass-topped table, reflecting her tiny puckered asshole back at him; her pelvis arching upward to take all of this thick cock into her.

"Cock! Cock! More cock!" she began to chant like some demented cheerleader. Then she began to moan with abandon, in ceaseless agony of delayed orgasm, as his giant cudgel pounded straight into her. Finally, she realized that they needed to be in a different position, so that he could get all of his length into her. She needed it to be deep, hard and punishing to bring her to the climax she so desired for future sanity.

Nina moaned in frustration, "Get on top of me on the table. I can't get enough of your cock," she demanded. Her husband clambered to the cold glass table top and went straight into her again as she pulled her legs up, flexing them up to her chest, her breasts being smashed flat, when he came down on her, pinning her to the mirrored table like a butterfly specimen. He rammed his great prick all the way home in her cunt, his balls slapping against the tiny brown ring of her anus below. "Clay! I can't come like this! Shove your finger in my asshole. Make me cum, darling! Oh hurry! I want you in my asshole, too! Hurry, my darling! Fill me!" Her husband became all the more inflamed as she kept asking him, urging him and demanding of him, rising to meeting his pounding cock in her loins. He reached under her, watching the reflection of him lifting her buttocks, easily, driving his prick rhythmically into the moistness of her ever-demanding cunt.

He located the crevice of her ass in the mirror and stretched it wide with his hands, searching for that softly pliant nether ring. Now, he located it with his middle finger and lewdly slipped the tip of it into her wildly flexing rectum, working it in, gradually, until he felt the muscle ring give a little. He pushed harder and the elastic flesh of her anus relaxed, his finger going in to the first knuckle. He felt the shock of it in her body as she recoiled instinctively, screwing her buttocks down and back, away from that punishing digit penetrating into her tight asshole.

"Come on, Clay. Push it in all the way! Right up my ass!" she screamed. Obediently, he jabbed his finger into her, all the way to the palm of his hand, reaching up into the sponginess of her rectum, burying it in her without mercy. "Aaah! It hurts! Ooooh! I love it!" she screeched. The compactly built former stripper screwed her ass back against his finger, and he moved it in her, twirling it around in the flesh depths of her back passage. He could feel his prick through the thin wall of tissue separating her vagina from her anal passage as his fat, hardened rod of flesh moved in and out of her.

Now, he began to move his finger in time to his cock, skewering her with both punishing instruments, reveling in the ecstasy of the dual ravishment. Nina mewled, gurgled, moaned and groaned with passion, the sounds coming from deep in her throat, interspersed with sharp gasps of pleasure as he rocked, smoothly, in and out of her cunt and wildly clenching tiny asshole simultaneously. Clay knew that she was nearing her climax, as she continued to mouth obscenities, driving him onward to greater effort, his own passion rising and spiraling toward the summit and a final thrusting, jabbing, spewing ejaculation. His cock became even harder and stiffer, growing to full blood-engorged erection, and he was painfully aware of the dammed up flood waiting to be released. She was wild, delirious and uncontrolled as she came nearer and nearer to her moment, that time of exquisite rapture.

"Oh fuck it! Fuck my cunt! Fuck my ass! Fuck me harder... oh, fuck... fuck me!" she chanted in wild abandon, increasing the speed, demanding her rightfully due orgasm, and she began the rushing, spiraling, giddy flight to the heights, where she felt as though she were a parachutist bailing out of a speeding airplane at fifteen thousand feet, and she was falling free, spinning free in a fall through space, the earth rushing up to meet her in climax; then gently, the brightly-hued umbrella of the parachute exploded over her head and floated her gently back to earth. It was as in a dream that she heard herself. Sounds belting out of her that formed no words just shrieks of pleasure.

As Nina screamed with the pleasure of her orgasm, Clay was spurred on to his own. He was in her, moving faster and faster, longer and harder and his hardened cock was like a machine, the piston of him moving in her with short, powerful strokes. He felt the load begin in his balls, pumping through the length of his penis, spewing in jerking jets of white viscous sperm far up into her cunt; while the spasms of pleasure shot through him in mind-shattering, body-reeling waves of sensuality. His cock continued to jump as he collapsed atop her with a huge groan of satiation.

"Jesus Christ!" he groaned. "I'm still coming..." In a few moments he rolled from atop her, his now flaccid prick pulling from her with a liquid, sucking sound, trailing a string of semen, as he crawled lazing from the discomfort of the glass table top where he had been able to see everything reflected back. He went over to the bar and poured two fresh martinis, bringing one to his wife, who, meanwhile had slipped off the table and was now reclining on the brocaded sofa. A vision of golden Oriental loveliness against the whiteness of the rich fabric made his cock begin to pound once more.

As he stretched out beside her, handing her a drink, she said, "You know I had a long talk with Jenna Harris this afternoon, dear." Marsdale was immediately interested. "

And what did my nosy little wife find out?" Nina inhaled deeply from her cigarette before she answered, "You just can't credit it, Clay, but that ravishingly beautiful girl has never had a decent fuck in her life. She doesn't get off on sex at all. I guess she's only been married a few months but it appears that husband of hers doesn't know what to do with that big hunk of meat of his."

"Well, I dare say, we can rectify that," he said leeringly, reaching out for his wife's pubic mound, still moist from the pleasant departure of a few moments before. Obscenely, Nina Marsdale opened her thighs wide to his exploring fingers, at the same time taking a large swallow of her martini.

Then, she said dreamily, "I'd like to teach that husband of hers a few things... oh, that hunk of meat, Clay! It's too wonderful! Can we go back and look at that videotape you made?"

"Sure, darling, just promise me you won't leave your old daddy for one of those newer models."

"Never," she said, giving him a long lingering kiss. Then, his rummaging fingers had found the bud of her clitoris, and he pressed the button of her sex, the explosion of sensation in her causing her to clamp her thighs tightly together, clamping his hand closely against her, heightening her pleasure. Then, her pelvis began to move in tiny circles of fully re-awakening desire.

"Oh, Clay, there will never be anyone else like you," she squealed, as she flung herself atop him, pinning his body to the couch, her lips and mouth avid upon him.

CHAPTER 4

Jenna Harris could not imagine how it was possible that Eddie could be staying out so late with two men discussing their tax issues. Usually, he shunned going out after hours with clients unless major billable hours were in the near future and this evening it just didn't make any sense that he would be out past midnight. She tried to wait up for him as she had read several articles on sexual techniques in marriage and she was eager to show her husband of three months that she was not an uptight little prude, but a loving responsive wife, willing to take pleasure and give pleasure. Finally, disappointed and worried about the future of her marriage, she had gone to bed; however, she could not sleep.

Her mind churned her thoughts into a morass of doubts and suspicions that threatened to drag her into the depths of despair. The more the worried wife tossed and turned and craved for the dark curtain of sleep to spread across the window of her mind, the more alert she became. After what seemed like hours, she resorted to her medicine cabinet's treasures where she took a sleeping pill. Long before her adulterous husband returned she was dead to the world in her narcotic induced sleep. Eddie was glad to see that she was asleep and he did not try to rouse her. Frankly for the first time since he'd married her he was relieved she was already knocked out from one of her little happy pills. Another young wife, however, had had a much more exciting evening.

Sally Dunn had gone to the tennis club at closing time where she had met Jenna's husband, Eddie. The two adulterers had fallen into each other's arms almost immediately, frantically, tearing at each other's clothing, exposing the softness and the hardness of flesh and blending them quickly in the headlong pursuit of their desperate need for satisfaction. The infinite maneuvers of their later lovemaking left them both sexually satiated and tingling with delirious mental, emotional and physical exhaustion. Then they had slept nude upon the sofa in the lobby of the darkened tennis club, and when they had awakened it was already two o'clock in the morning.

"Suffering Christ!" he exclaimed, looking at his phone. "It's two o'clock!"

Sally unconcerned crept closer into his arms, snuggling against him and reaching down between them to caress his flaccid cock, in an attempt to arouse him once more.

"Kiss me," she murmured low and throaty.

Briefly, Eddie kissed her with cool lips, breaking away before tongues were entwined to say, "Sally, for God's sake! We've got to get out of here. What would your husband say and my wife is going to kill me."

Dreamily Sally offered, "Oh, David's not expecting me. He's playing in that tournament so I told him I was going to stay with my sister. The time's not important to me."

"Well, why the hell didn't you tell me before," he said in a slightly irritated fashion. "We could have gone to a motel or something and I would have made up an excuse for Jenna."

Sally Dunn merely ignored his annoyance. She wasn't interested in a petty lecture. There was a big cock at her disposal and she wanted more of it and she would not be detoured from her destination. The pert brunette rolled over on top of him and ground her pelvis down on him, forcing his limp prick to lie in the furrow of her cock-hungry, insatiable cunt while she moved her hips lewdly, demandingly; meanwhile, using her lips and mouth on his body. As man of the world he pretended to be, Eddie was not in fact that knowledgeable when it came to sex. He would not have believed that he was capable of another sexual bout so soon, but his immense cock began to engorge with blood, rising and jerking into the moistness of her well-educated pussy-lips.

As soon as she felt the first throbbing of his erection, she slid off him, gripped his big cock in her hands, milking the foreskin back and sucked him to hardened readiness, flopping to her back to take him into her with her legs pulled up to her chest and reveling in the gigantic hunk of pulsating flesh he was sinking into her cunt. Then, he went into her with long, slow and deliberate strokes, his ejaculation and climax delayed, he brought her to orgasm until finally she was completely spent, satiated from the unending pleasure of it. Sally lay on her back, unable to gather the strength to ease him, bring him completion, and he was frantic, fucking into her nonresponding cunt, unable to come again he was so uptight. Pulling out of her, he knelt over her lips, forcing her to take his aching cock into her mouth. She nibbled on it, finally taking all of him to suck while he moved his pelvis in a motion over her face, forcing her to take even more of him on each down stroke, making her gag as it drove to the back of her throat, her lips turning in as she absorbed him without complaint; while, on the outstroke, her lips pulled out, the pink, inner parts of her mouth showing.

It was hard work, but finally the boiling sperm came hosing through the length of him, spewing the viscous, white semen thickly into her mouth. She kept swallowing until all of the sticky juice was siphoned from his jerking cock and consumed. Then, he rolled heavily to his side and slept beside her. The next time they awakened it was an hour later and they dressed themselves hurriedly in silent exhaustion; both of them totally spent. Jenna Harris got up the next day with a sleeping pill hangover and the fervent hope that her husband would have some explanation for his errant ways. No such explanation was forthcoming. Eddie slept until almost noon as he had the day off and didn't even so much as mention the lateness of his arrival home the previous evening. Jenna tried to be as pleasant as possible under the circumstances but her husband seemed to be ignoring her. When finally, he picked up car keys and abstractly waved good-bye without kissing her, she feared the worst. It was the first time in the three months since they had been married that he had failed to kiss her good-bye and to the already fearful, suspicious wife it was almost a sign that it was all over.

The gnawing question in her mind surfaced suddenly, punching her in the gut with its intensity. What if Eddie's already found another woman? Someone to do all those horrible perverted things with him that she was incapable of; what would she do? If Eddie divorced her she only had two options, her grandmother who would tell her to snap out of it and get a job or her parents that would suffocate her with readings from the Book of Mormon until they found her a suitable husband. Jenna didn't know that she was the third of three wives that evening in what was turning into a little circle. Unfortunately, she was the only one out of the three, since both Nina Marsdale and Sally Dunn had a wildly satisfying bout of sexual ecstasy. Jenna didn't know that she was the only one hanging out there in sexual frustration she only knew that something was dreadfully wrong and she wanted the score to change. She loved her husband but she feared divorce more than anything. She couldn't go back to Salt Lake and she would be damned if she had to take some low paying job. The high life of a corporate lawyer's wife came with lots of perks and Jenna liked the lifestyle her husband's money provided her.

CHAPTER 5

Eddie drove to his afternoon hand-ball session ready to play with another client but in reality unable to concentrate on anything but the memory of the wild night of uninhibited sex with Sally Dunn. He could still feel her lips around his cock sucking him dry as he parked his car. She had sucked every last ounce of sperm from his cock like she was dehydrated in the desert.

Suddenly the woman that he could see in his mind's eye stuck her head out of the rear of the pro shop and called, "Eddie, you're wanted on the telephone."

"Okay, Sally, thanks," he called loping across the parking lot to the telephone in the pro shop.

"Yes," he said into the telephone, "Eddie Harris here."

"Eddie its Nina Marsdale. I'd like to have a little talk with you today. I didn't know your cell number so I hope you don't mind me ringing the Pro shop to see if you were coming in today. What's your schedule look like?"

"Well, let's see," he said uncertainly. What the hell did Nina Marsdale want with him? "I have a client in a couple of minutes at one, I think that's it unless he wants to have dinner after; I should be through here by four at the latest. What is it?"

"I don't wish to discuss it on the telephone, Eddie. Why don't you meet me for a drink about four. How about the Carlton Hill Hotel cocktail lounge?" The mysterious tone of her voice and the urgency she projected to him, her words surging through his consciousness, held him absolutely intrigued.

"Well, all right, Mrs. Marsdale, if it's important, I'll be there. Carlton Hill at four."

"That's a good little boy!" she said and then she hung up. "Did I hear correctly?" Eddie asked himself stunned that the wife of his former boss would be so flippant with him. After all Clay still had a hand in at the office but he was essentially retired. So why in the world would his wife even want to speak to him? Unless she was doing some kind of tax dodge behind Clay's back he couldn't think of any reason. He didn't have time to dwell on it. He had a client to lose to after ensuring that he nearly beat him. God knows they loved it when they won after a hard battle never knowing Eddie tossed in the towel to sop their egos before going over their legal troubles. Ugh. Jenna. She wouldn't be happy about last night.

Then there would be the matter of breaking the news that he wouldn't be home again this evening to her- that would piss her off for sure but then she was never happy so at this point he wasn't gonna sweat her ice queen problems. Things were certainly getting busy for the Eddie and he loved it. After losing by the nearest of margins to a very happy client he pointed him off to the showers then he called his wife.

"Jenna," he said. "I won't be back for dinner tonight. They're having a board meeting and deciding whether they can expand the club facilities and I as sit on the finance committee I have to be here. I don't know how late it's going to be so don't hold dinner and don't wait up for me."

She was instantly suspicious. Two late nights in a row, just what was happening with her husband? But she still felt a bit foolish about thwarting her husband's advances and she didn't want to start a row so she choked back the angry tirade that threatened to rush forth from her mouth.

"Okay, Eddie," was all she could manage. "I love you."

"Oh, Jenna, I love you too. Now don't go getting all worked up because we're separated once in a while. Why don't you call up one of your friends and go to the movies or something?" he said trying to distract her from his guilt.

"Maybe I will," she said none too convincingly. "See you later, dear."

For some reason after his client shook hands and agreed to Eddie's ideas for his tax shelters. Eddie didn't just take a quick shower. He didn't give it a lot of thought but before his meeting with Nina Marsdale, Eddie took a long soothing shower and shaved. He patted on some after shave he kept in his locker and carefully dried his hair. Now, he was glad that he had as he sat side by side with Nina Marsdale in a booth in the dimly lit cocktail lounge of the Carlton Hill Hotel. Eddie decided to have the same drink that Nina ordered, a dry martini, and over their drinks they sat chatting of trivialities as they became acquainted with each other. Eddie was struck by the petite, yet exotic beauty of the woman. There was the Oriental mystery of her slanted eyes, her jet black hair cut in a precision style flattering to straight hair, the fashionable fit of her dress, revealing her petite perfect body, the vivacity of her smile, and her animated stimulating conversation. Why had she chosen this place to talk to him and what was it she wanted to talk to him about, for she still had not revealed to him an inkling of the nature of their meeting.

"Eddie," she suddenly became serious, "what are your future plans at Firm? Do you aim for a senior partnership or are you going to be content with just a junior position?"

Wary now and even slightly angry at her boldness, he said, "Are those loaded questions?"

"Well, I haven't told a single soul this, but I expect that with my track record and the steadily increase in billable hours I bring in that it would only be proper that eventually I would be offered a promotion. So yes in answer to your question I would like a future with the Firm, definitely."

Nina listened attentively, and then cut in, "So you do have some ambition?"

"Yes, I suppose so," he said, "don't most of us want to get somewhere in life."

"And what do you want out of life, Eddie? Surely more than just a chance at a new senior position."

"Well, I'd like to have a family. Of course, Jenna and I have only been married for a couple of months but..."

"But what... you're not having such great luck in the sack, is that it?" she asked dropping the bombshell on all the previously innocuous conversation. Eddie nearly shit and for a second stared at her open mouthed, not knowing what this woman was getting at... what was she hinting at?

"Why it's not a problem only that Jenna is from a very religious Mormon background and she's a little uptight, but we're working it out." He would have put in entirely different terms but he didn't dare. She could put a bug up her husband's ass and Eddie would find himself doing dog's body work around the office. No more fancy clients, no more dinners out on the firm's dollar, hell no more anything if he wasn't careful.

"And while you're working it out," she questioned a lewd little smile playing about her lips, "you've found some new outlets for your sexual frustration?" He was really getting hot under the collar now. How dare this woman who was practically a stranger to him make these insinuations.

"Just what are you driving at Mrs. Marsdale," he asked coldly.

"Don't be coy, stud," she whispered hoarsely, "I saw a little video of you and Sally Dunn with your cock rammed down her throat. Now I don't know whether you're aware of it up 'til now but at Marina we usually share and share alike."

"Jesus Christ!" he gasped a scarlet flush creeping up from his neck. Then he saw the smoky light smoldering in her almond shaped eyes and he guessed what was going to be her next pitch.

"What do you want with me, Mrs. Marsdale?" he asked already knowing the answer.

"You, stud," she said, her voice low, throaty, sexy, placing a hand on his thigh and moving it in small massaging circles inching upward to his cock. Eddie's prick was instantly alert, the blood racing to engorge it, his scrotum tightening below, as her hand caressed him, making him feel that he was in some kind of weird dream. It couldn't be reality. How could reality be his boss's wife sitting at a booth in a cocktail lounge massaging his cock to a throbbing, jerking, almost instantaneous erection when he hardly knew her?

"Me? Are you sure?" he said stupidly with the excitement rising in him. "I mean, you're Clay's wife and all..." Her eyes rolled upward and she stated coolly.

"Clay and I are adults. He has his affairs and I have mine. The arrangement works out beautifully."

"But what about the tape?" he asked. "Don't worry about it, there's a lot of tape floating around the club that has nothing to do with poor volleying on the part of the new students. There are other things to occupy your mind, now."

He reached for her thigh, lying warmly beside his, but she put him off with a gentle hand.

"Not yet," she warned, her eyes promising him a future with her that looked very, very rosy. "We can get a room here."

"Okay, let's do it!" he said huskily. Holy shit! Had he said that? Yup because just like that she left and said, "Follow me young man." Instantly, they rose, threading their way through the lounge; he grateful for the subdued lighting, as he walked with his hand in his pockets, trying to hide the obvious bulge of his hardened erect cock, inside his pants. In minutes they had gone through the farce of registration with a disinterested hotel clerk and found themselves in a rather plush suite. As they walked to the elevator she flicked a glance back over her shoulder at him and burbled, "Smart boy, Eddie. This bodes well for your long term future. Make me happy and that makes my husband happy. Get it?"

He just nodded his head in reply. His brain too overloaded to actually form words. Eddie was to find this a day of surprises for the Mrs. Marsdale went straight to the telephone and ordered room service to bring up a bottle and a cocktail shaker. It was obvious to the young man that Nina had done this kind of thing before. As she went into the bathroom he watched the ripple of her buttocks under the tight dress, her thighs clearly outlined under the tight material, the contour of her body exciting him, and he felt the familiar surge of blood into his cock. Christ! He'd never had a Chinese woman before. He answered the knock on the door and let in the room service clerk who was wheeling a cart with ice bucket, bottles and glasses. He tipped the man not daring to look at the bill he had just signed. Shit! What the fuck am I doing here in this swanky hotel with my boss's wife? This little setup is going to cost me a week's wages. I'm really flipping out. First, Sally Dunn and now Nina Marsdale but its Nina that can really jeopardize my job even though she was the one that initiated this whole thing. And what about Jenna? This is hardly fair to her. We've only been married for three months, for Christ's sake and already I'm screwing around on her like mad.

Eddie was so caught up in his guilty thoughts that he had not even realized that his boss's wife was back in the living room of the hotel suite, until her voice came to him from the center of the room. Apparently, she had taken it upon herself to mix the drinks already and now she had two glasses in her hands as she moved toward him.

"You didn't have to wait for me. You could have done the drinks," she said. Silently, he took the glass from her hands. Her words meant nothing to him. He could only stand and stare at her dumbly. She was incredibly beautiful. She wore a tightly fitted, floor length, Oriental costume of white silk brocade, shining dully in the soft glow from the muted lights of the big room. The dress shimmered and played over her body as she walked sensuously toward him, and he saw that the garment was split from floor to waist, exposing and hiding her legs alternately with each step. There was something forbidden but exciting about the high, mandarin collar that enfolded her neck, covering her chastely as indeed, the entire dress did, except for this sleekly trim legs which were hidden from his view entirely, only when she stopped before him. Nina stood, looking up at him, the smokiness in her almond-shaped eyes revealing her mood. She reached out to put a hand on his athletically muscular arm.

"Eddie, I'm so glad that you could meet me," she said a trifle breathlessly in that sing-song voice of hers.

"So am I, but I'm... uh... a little embarrassed about this. I mean even what you said about Clay and his affairs... and all... still..."

"For God's sake, Eddie. Let's get over that shall we. I didn't come up here to discuss our respective spouses. That would be too dull for words. Now let's make a little excitement, shall we?" she said after her eyes glimmering like two hot slits.

"Agreed," he said. Nina sank gracefully to the floor pulling the cushions from the sofa onto the floor to sit on. She arranged herself on the pillow with her legs tucked underneath and sipped her drink and motioned for him to sit beside her. Eddie took a huge swallow from his glass and sat down awkwardly on the floor. He wondered, as he lowered himself, whether or not she would have anything on under that fabulous dress she wore.

"What a lovely dress," he said. "Thank you. I bought it this afternoon when I knew I was going to be seeing you."

"Oh, Nina," he groaned, "you're fabulous. I want you so much. I can't help myself." With that he reached for her and she came eagerly into his arms, her lips searching for and finding his. Their mouths welded together and their tongues probed, tasting, savoring and exciting each other. His big hands explored her small, exquisite body; her curves under the material of the dress he found unencumbered by other garments. He felt her breasts, massaged them, feeling their smooth firmness under his hand and reveling in the feel of them, wanted them free and naked in his hands now. Upwardly, his hand slid on her back to her neck, found the zipper, grasped it and gave a long smooth pull to her waist. She shrugged her shoulders and the garment fell forward, exposing her whole body to the navel. He feasted his eyes for a moment upon the golden loveliness of her. Instantly, his mouth was on her, kissing and caressing those magnificent, mounding orbs of her femaleness, as his hands kneaded her, grasping a nipple and teasing it to erectness in his fingers. The Asian beauty lay back upon the cushions forcing him to follow. With a deft movement she removed the dress from her hips and legs, and she was completely nude before his lustful gaze, the swell of her hips, the long tapering legs, those supple dancer's legs, exciting him even more.

His cock jerked inside his trousers, making its bid for freedom. "Let's get those clothes off of you," she said. Her small, cool hands were efficient, they moved with sure knowledge on his body, and he was soon stripped of his clothing, revealing his manhood, stiffly alert, throbbing and engorged.

"Fantastic!" she said, reaching out to fondle the hardness and length of him, moving the slack skin, experimentally to expose the blood-red head; then she lay back, suddenly, pulling him on top of her. His cock came naturally to rest in the soft, hair-lined furrow of her cunt as she captured it, forcing the length of him to lie huge and thick against her, its pressure seeming to arouse her instantly.

"Do you want to fuck me?" she asked.

"Christ, yes!" he gasped, his breath beginning to come heavily, labored.

"Well tell me, then. Tell me what you want to do!"

"I really want to fuck, Nina," he said, his rough hands digging into both her breasts, squeezing them through his fingers like they were bread dough.

"How do you want it? How do you want to fuck me?" she hissed lasciviously into his ear.

"I want to fuck you so you scream for more!"

Eddie vowed with intensity.

"Yes, baby. Kill me with your big cock! Fuck me hard till I scream!" she whispered hoarsely.

"Oh, yes, yes, baby, baby," he grunted, trying to recapture her lips.

"You'll do anything I want?" she queried, her eyes closed, breath coming in little short gasps.

"Anything you want... anything," Eddie promised.

"Then do it now!" she said, a moan coming deeply from her throat. "Fuck me! Ram your gigantic piece of meat into my cunt and fuck me like you've never fucked before! Fuck me now!" And with that, Nina raised her legs, obscenely flexing them, and reached down between their loins to grip his huge, blood-engorged prick in her tiny hand, guiding it expertly between the lips of her warmly ready pussy, where she moved the knob of it up and down in the moist furrow, parting the soft, dark hair of the vaginal opening with the throbbing cudgel and moving the foreskin back and forth several times, until he felt it grow even harder in her hand. He could wait no more. Firmly, with demanding pressure, he moved his hips against her. She felt the strength of him and placed the cowled head of his cock at the cunt-lipped opening of her, the tip of it resting just inside. She was ready for him now, and he drove his gargantuan rod of flesh long, deep and hard into her female softness.

"Oh... Eddie... oh!" she groaned beneath him as he felt the vaginal muscles give way with the onslaught and his cock was in her carnal canal, the warm, elastic, inner lining slipping wetly along his length, clinging to his hardened flesh, clasping him, claiming him and absorbing him to the hilt, his testicles swinging below, slapped against the cheeks of her upturned buttocks, as he rammed the giant phallus into her throbbing, wide split cleft without mercy. She screamed with the first entry of it, as Eddie struck bottom, his cock flicking past her cervix. Her hips twisted under him, screwing them back and down to escape the sudden penetration; but, he thrust all the harder into her, trying to cram the last bit of his massive prick up into her soft, pliant pussy.

Momentarily, he stopped, letting her cunt adjust to him, resting on top of her with his huge, fleshy rod skewering her to the floor. She opened her eyes wide, smiling smokily up at him now, the feeling of being stuffed once again with cock pleasing her immensely.

"Oh, you're so huge," she moaned. "I adore it. It's so marvelous to have a big cock in my cunt!" Her hips began to move under him, then; first, in tiny circles, tantalizingly, changing to longer back and forth strokes, screwing her ass back, forcing withdrawal, only to move forward again, her cunt sliding and climbing up his giant pole, as she impaled herself fully on the thick length of him; finally, she moved with wildly gyrating buttocks, the smoldering sensuality blown to a raging furnace in her crotch. The adulterous husband was in a rapture of his own. Eddie felt the fire of her, the wonderful feeling of her moist, clasping pussy moving around him driving him wild. He braced himself on his knees and elbows above her wildly thrashing body, letting her hungry cunt slither itself up and down the rigid length of his cock at will. A couple of times he bucked forward on her upstroke, driving the growing head of his member almost through the back wall of her womb.

Then he began to move with her, grinding his pelvis onto hers, his cock moving in and out rhythmically, and she strained back at him, finally matching her movements to his, so that he pistoned her smoothly. Nina moaned in ecstasy beneath him, welcoming his pounding pelvis, lifting her ass up to him, arching off the floor to meet him, her legs opening and closing around his waist, fucking back at his rampaging prick in the chanting rhythm of sexual surrender.

"Harder... deeper... fuck me... fuck me... harder... come on... deeper... get in farther... farther in my pussy. I want to feel you rub my spine Do it!" Her words bit into him, driving him on to plunging insanity, as he fucked into her, ramming and cramming with redoubled effort. Nina's mouth gaped open and her head flailed from side to side as he went in deeper, faster, his cock growing each moment, filling her sugar sweet tunnel with its rock-hard maleness. He pulled her knees up to her chest, her crotch exposed, vulnerable, inviting him to plumb her sexual depths. "I want more! More cock! Let's do something different!" she gasped. "Just tell me what you want," he panted.

"Come, my big handsome stud, let me up and I'll teach you a new way to fuck!" she promised. He pulled out of her and rolled to his side, as she scrambled lithely to her knees, kneeling on a soft pillow, presenting her with her luscious backside, waggling it in his face teasingly. He could see the slightly spread lips of her softly hair-lined pussy smiling at him, and above, the tight puckered ring of her asshole was beckoning lasciviously to him.

Her voice was shaky. "Kneel behind me, Eddie!"

Excitedly, he moved into position, his cock jutting impatiently out toward the soft, quivering crevice. She reached back between her legs and grasped his prick, guiding it to her cunt lips where she dipped the head of it in the moistness of her, lubricating it well; then she moved the great blood-engorged tip to the entrance of her tiny, brownish-colored anus, smearing the viscous liquid on that opening to prepare it for his giant-sized spear's penetration.

"Spread my asscheeks with your hands. I'll guide your cock in my ass!" she whispered. Eddie reached down, grasping a smooth, trembling cheek in each hand and carefully spread them apart, revealing the vulnerable brown opening of her tight, flexing anal passage.

"Now, gently, slowly, put it into my ass," she instructed him with baited, excited breath. Softly, with her fingers she pressed the large, smooth head against the rubber nether ring and he strained, moving slowly and with constant and increasing force, until with a faint popping noise, the head slipped in and he could feel the tantalizing, elastic muscles clasping him strongly, the tight, yet soft, sponginess of her back passage giving him a series of sensations that he had never before experienced. His sensitive flesh was trapped, almost painfully; then he felt her anus begin to relax inside.

"Okay! Shove it in all the way. But slowly, do it slowly!" she hissed at him, lowering her shoulders to a cushion and swiveling her head to look back at him. Eddie flexed his pelvis and shoved harder, the length and breadth of his cock disappearing completely inside. Instinctively he paused not moving to allow time for her rear passage to adjust to his invasion.

"No-no, too fast, go easy... now... pull it out... all the way out," she said with excitement mounting in her voice. The mammoth member came out of her with a rush, and she expertly lowered it to her cunt lips.

"Okay, now inside my cunt..." Willing to go along with her exciting game, he moved forward, burying his thickness deep up into the straining moistness of her pussy. "Now, back in my asshole... and then back in my cunt... oh. Eddie... fuck me... fuck me... fuck me..." Eddie needed no further instructions from his Oriental seductress. He pulled from her cunt and she guided it to her anus again. This time it went in smoothly. She was more relaxed, and he rammed it in with wild ecstatic abandon. The woman gasped with pleasure as he pulled from her, she guiding the cock to her cunt, where he plunged his cock in her to the hilt, his balls slapping resoundingly into the soft, inner smoothness of her thighs. Now the pattern was established.

He began to move in and out of her, alternating between anus and vagina, long rampaging strokes, backed by his powerful legs and pelvis, and she guided it with accuracy in the alternation, screwing her hips back at him to get deeper penetration in each orifice. Nina mewled, gurgled and groaned, the sounds coming from deep in her throat, interspersed with sharp gasps of pleasure as his mighty ramrod of flesh pistoned in and out of her cunt and asshole. She was approaching her orgasm, her breath came in fitful jerks, as he moved in and out of both hungry holes, the sensations engulfing and consuming her, and she was filled and fulfilled, the dizzying heights of her climax visible to her as that magnificent stem of hardened lust ravished her almost beyond endurance...

"Yes... it's marvelous... its heaven... fuck... fuck..." she panted in rhythm, chanting a sexual litany."In my ass... in my cunt... in my ass... in my cunt... fuck me... fuck me... fuck me." She was practically screaming now, faster and faster she chanted to him, demanding her climax, wanting it to come, but wanting it to go on forever, too. In moments she was transported to the fiery brink of a volcanic crater, the smoking, steamy heat of it enveloping her, searing into her loins, flaming through her mind, until with a groan her orgasm released her in spasms of pleasurable euphoria, and she floated through space, down, down into the burning depths of her sexual pleasure. Surprisingly, to her lust-crazed mind, she was not burned at all. Her release came and she was in the hotel suite, on the floor, Eddie's cock still plunging into her with relentless force.

"Oh. God... Jesus..... I'm coming." she screamed in sensual agony of orgasmic ecstasy. As Nina screamed, Eddie knew that he was near himself. He grabbed her by the hips and pulled her hard back against him.

He was up her asshole, and he kept his cock there, moving faster, longer and harder into her straining, tightly clenching back passage, ramming into her, the sensations in him growing ever more intense. He could feel the beginnings of his own ejaculation, as his hardened flesh fucked into her like a well-oiled machine, the piston of him moving in her cylinder with increasing power. Now, his sperm-loaded balls began to jerk, the pumping action evident of the length of his penis. Suddenly, it was there, spewing in hosing jets of white, viscous semen far up into her rectum, while spasms of pure, animalistic pleasure shot through him, flashing in electric jolts through his mind and shuddering through his body in wave after wave of nerve-tingling sexuality. His cock continued to pump for several moments as he collapsed on top of her, lying on her back, prone, as she lay under him on her stomach.

"My God," he said hoarsely, panting for breath, "I've never had anything like that!"

"Mmm... you like... huh?" she asked.

"I've never had a woman like you," he said, his prick still jerking in her, "It was just the most fabulous thing I've ever had."

"Well, we have plenty of other things to try too," she promised. "That is, of course, if you're interested."

"Interested!" he said without hesitation. "I'll be your slave if you'll do that again." With those words he rolled from atop her, retrieved their drinks, lit cigarettes for them, and they stretched out comfortably on the cushions in front of the window. Clay Marsdale had been in the bathroom all the time, playing with his new toy, the spy camera. Fortunately, Nina had maneuvered his young employee onto the floor so all their grunts and groans of sexual abandon would be picked up by the small floor mike concealed by the leg of the sofa. Obviously, both of them were satiated and that made Clay happy too. Voyeurism was one of his favorite diversions. Jesus Christ, he thought, my little wife is some woman. No wonder I'm never bored. I've never known a woman who likes to fuck as much as my little Oriental firecracker. She'd have a cock in her twenty-four hours a day if she could. In her ass... her cunt... her mouth...I am one lucky bastard! Shit! I hope she's coming home soon. I've got a big hard cock I want to ram into her myself. I don't think Eddie Harris needs to have a three-way laid on him right now although Nina certainly likes to have two cocks in her. The director of the Marina Tennis Clinic and retired senior partner of the biggest west coast law firm in California stretched out on the floor of the bathroom partially in the hallway of the suite just in time to see Nina's lips encircling Eddie's cock, manipulating him to flesh-hardened, blood-engorged readiness. I guess I'll just have to concentrate on what it's going to be like when I fuck Eddie's wife, he thought taking his own raging hard on in hand.

CHAPTER 6

Jenna had not wanted to wait up for Eddie but she could not sleep and the sleeping pill she had taken the other night made her feel so groggy the next day that she did not want to go through that again. She tossed and turned and tossed so more, every few moments looking at the clock which seemed almost to have stopped, time was going so slowly. Finally at 5AM when she could see a little bit of daylight beginning to filter through the bedroom drapes, she heard him. She was too distraught for a confrontation with her husband so she feigned sleep; although she laid under the blankets like a coiled spring, listening to him undress. After what seemed like hours, Eddie crawled into bed beside her. Jenna lay still for nearly ten agonizing minutes until she heard soft snores pass his lips. Still pretending that she was sound asleep, restlessly, she moved closer to him, snuggling into his back and throwing an arm over his body. Eddie turned away, gently removing her arm, and moved away to his side of the king-sized bed. Feeling like she had been punched in the stomach by his unconscious rejection of her, Jenna smothered her face in the pillow and tried to keep from screaming out her sorrow.

The next day there was to be some sort of open house at the tennis club for new members which Jenna had planned to attend. It seemed all the wives hung out at least part of the day at the club so she had reluctantly joined thinking it would boost her social standing. Eddie woke and rolled over seeing the other side of the bed empty. He rose and went downstairs to make his protein drink in the blender. Jenna was sitting in the kitchen, tensely, going over the newspaper with blank eyes and she did not greet him when he came into the kitchen. Complete silence reigned although the atmosphere was charged with vibrations so heavy they could have been sliced and packaged.

Eddie dressed and almost left the house without saying goodbye when he remembered something. At the door he paused still looking out at the driveway one hand on the knob. Without even the courtesy of turning to face her he said,"Oh, by the way, Jenna, don't forget we're going over to the Marsdale's tonight."

"Okay," she said, not looking up from her paper. Then he was gone. Jenna got up and watched him until he was out of sight, then she opened the door and slammed it shut out of sheer frustration. She stumbled up to her bedroom in a fit of rage. At least he could have the decency to let me know what he's up to, she fumed. I am owed some kind of explanation for his behavior the last week. If it's another woman, I want to know. I have the right to know. Realizing that she was hardly going to solve any of her problems by lying in bed, she decided to busy herself with some of the things she had been putting off. Still angry, she began wandering around the house picking up the dirty clothes to take to the laundry.

In the bathroom hamper she found one of Eddie's gym shirts and covering the little polo player in the corner was a big smear of red lipstick! Jenna thought she almost could have rationalized that lipstick. It could have been anything but she couldn't think of what 'anything' could be. Then she found the hardened, thick glob on the inside of his shorts that convicted him in her mind. She stared at the whitish blob of his dried semen and knew now without a doubt that he had been with another woman! Eddie, her husband of three months was fucking around! Once again, feeling like she had been punched in the stomach, Jenna wondered just how much she could stand. Dully, she walked over to the sofa, not feeling like taking her husband's sex-stained laundry to the cleaners but not knowing what else to do. It never even occurred to her that she could just use the washing machine in her own house. Dully, her eyes fixed themselves on the small bar. She went to it, like a magnet poured herself a stiff tumbler of scotch and drank it off in four gulps, feeling the fiery liquid boil into her guts, numbing her brain and tingling through her tense body. She wanted to stop the raging thoughts; push them into oblivion, anything to blot out the memory, the knowledge that her husband was already involved in an affair with another woman after only a few months of marriage.

Jenna was confident of her looks, indeed she knew that she was beautiful and desirable. As if to check, she went into the bathroom, removed her robe and looked at herself in the full-length mirror. Critically, she examined her reflection, smoothing her hands over generous breasts and the swell of hips and thighs, turning to look at the rounded, firm buttocks and finding no flaw in her svelte figure. She knew that she was fully developed, feminine and capable of much love. Now, she examined the soft, fleecy triangle of her pubic mound, turned to examine, in turn, the tight split of her vaginal opening; finally, standing again, using her hands to pull up her breasts to full mounds of femaleness, trying to pose provocatively, lewdly, obscenely. She found the poses totally alien to her character. Her own face came back into focus and she was startled for a second. She had been sick with worry and her face showed it. What am I going to do? How will I live if he throws me out? Like starving rats horrible thoughts of self-pity raced through her mind, skittering this way and that but never stopping long enough to let her see her problems were all to be laid at her own feet.

Suddenly the front doorbell sounded and Jenna barely hesitated. She certainly was not in the mood for any company but she did not want to be caught in the middle of the day still in her bathrobe. Hurriedly, she grabbed a summer shift from the closet, shrugging it on over her and smoothing it down over her hips and breasts not bothering to put on panties or a bra. Rapidly, she ran a brush through her golden hair and went to answer the front door. Standing there his hands on his hips not in his usual tennis garb was Clay Marsdale, her husband's former boss. It seemed to Jenna that since Clay had taken 'early' retirement last year he spent all his time at the club playing tennis like some fanatic. She blinked and realized this was the first time she could recall outside the firm she had seen him anything other than tennis clothes. She was startled. "Why, Mr. Marsdale, what can I do for you? Eddie's already gone and I'm about to head over to the open house."

"I didn't come here to see Eddie," he said in a very stern sounding voice. "May I come in? It's important."

"Oh, certainly," she swung the door wide for him. "Please come in. Forgive me. I'm a little out of it today," she said, stumbling over her words.

Marsdale entered and sat down on the edge of a chair and refused her offer for refreshment, liquid or otherwise.

"Something very important has come up," he said in a very menacing tone. Jenna was really mystified. Why would Clay Marsdale have anything important to discuss with her?

"What is it, Mr. Marsdale?" she began. Worriedly, she sank down on the sofa, being careful of the manner of her sitting, aware that she had no underwear on in front of this strange man. Clay leered at her barely able to conceal his lust. His eyes had caught the fact that she was not wearing anything underneath her summer shift; additionally, he had caught the smell of liquor on her breath, and he knew that all was not well in the Harris household.

"Mrs. Harris, there's no need now for beating about the bush," he said his lips pulling back into a tight line. "No doubt, you are aware of the fact that your husband did not arrive home until almost daylight and that he probably offered no explanation for his behavior. I can tell you that at this moment his future with the firm is in serious jeopardy."

Jenna gasped and covered her face from him with acute humiliation. She didn't answer him. Dear God, did everyone know about Eddie's infidelity except her? As usual Jenna only heard what she wanted. She heard him say her husband was cheating but the fact that he might soon be out of job and she would be cast aside with him fell on deaf ears.

"You know, don't you?" his voice was harsh, demanding.

"Yes," she said dully.

"Do you have any idea where he was during those long hours away from you?" he probed unmercifully, acting like some kind of inquisitor of prisoners. "No, I don't," her voice squeaked out.

"I know where he was!" He had waited quietly for a couple of moments before dropping his bombshell. Jenna's reaction was immediate. Her head jerked up. She stared in horror, her face a mask of stunned hopelessness.

"Where... how can you know?"

"I know where your husband was BECAUSE HE WAS WITH MY WIFE, NINA!" The young blonde wished at that moment that a hole would open in her living room floor so she could be swallowed up and would not have to face this shock and embarrassment. She again covered her shamed face with her hands, blocking her from his leering gaze.

"With Nina... your wife?" she stuttered out almost inaudibly from behind her hands.

"Yes, in fact, I filmed the entire thing on video

and I want you to come over to my house to see it," he said.

"Dear God, no!" she cried and flung herself down on the couch, her dress rising with her movement to reveal her long, smoothly tapering legs to the lustful gaze of Clay Marsdale. He allowed her to stay that way for a few moments, and then went to sit beside her on the couch to soothe her with words of sympathy.

"Now, now, Mrs. Harris. I know how you must feel. How shocking it is to find out that your husband has been unfaithful." Then, gently, he raised her up, continuing. "But you must remember that I've been cuckolded too. My own wife was with your husband!"

"Of course, you're right," she murmured, "I'd almost forgotten."

"Now, Mrs. Harris, I don't know what you propose to do about your husband, but I assure you that I am going to take some kind of action and soon!" he said, almost frightening her with the force of his words. Uncertainty and confusion were swirling through her. She did not want to have to make decisions at a time like this.

"I just don't know. I need some time to think..." her words trickled off as her mind hit overload.

Marsdale continued on. "I've had a little more time to think about it. I'm not at all sure that I want to divorce my wife for her... uh... indiscretion. I don't want to go through that at this time. But, I must say that the need for revenge is strong in me. And of course there is the matter of your husband's future with the firm."

Jenna stared at him, wide-eyed, not understanding what he was driving at. "What do you mean?" she asked.

"I think that we should pay them back. I think that they should know what it's like to have the same thing done to them!" He smiled at her suggestively, lewdly, his voice taking on a seductive tone. Jenna turned crimson, fully understanding his proposal now.

"Why, Mr. Marsdale, that's absolutely outrageous. I'm not interested in pursuing that line at all."

"But that's the only way that we can make them see the light. Make them confront themselves to know if they really care. It's the only way of getting back our partners," he purred. His reasoning escaped her, but his smooth convincing presentation of the idea seemed somewhat of a solution. She couldn't agree with him, but neither could she really have any way of knowing what to do in a situation like this where she had no experience. After all, Eddie had certainly broken their marriage vows. But two wrongs do not make a right.

"Oh, Mr. Marsdale, maybe what you say is right. I don't know," she said doubtfully.

"Of course, I'm right," he stated firmly. "Now, let's have a little drink. I feel so uptight, I need something to relax."

"I don't think so." she began. "Oh come on, Mrs. Harris. You do have a drink every once in a while don't you?" he asked, his gaze penetrating her. He knows. He can smell the scotch I had before he came.

"Okay, what'll be?" he asked, automatically going for the bar and then stopping, "with your permission, of course."

"Go ahead, Mr. Marsdale," she said her voice disinterested, lifeless, now all thoughts on her husband's adultery.

"Maybe we can get a little less formal. My name's Clay. May I call you Jenna? I hope if we are contemplating some plan of action we are at least going to be on a first name basis."

The clueless wife was really shocked now. "You don't really mean that you're considering... what you suggested... intimated... before...?"

"I don't see why not?" he leered. "What's sauce for the goose is also good for the gander, don't you know. Then there is always the possibility that if I made a condition of your husband's continuing employment," he shrugged leaving the rest unsaid. She was visibly disturbed.

She had no intention of pretending or otherwise to be an adulterous whore. Marsdale poured some stiff drinks and brought one over to her. They sat and chatted while Jenna nervously sipped the glass of straight scotch, and before she knew it the glass was empty. Clay watched her closely. He moved in quickly. "Another drink, my dear?" he asked.

"No, thanks. I rarely drink. Well, all right, but just a small one this time, it's still afternoon." The scotch was beginning to make her feel a little reckless; additionally a small bolt of electrical energy had balled itself, racing through her body, along her nerve endings to unleash its force in a gigantic stab at her genitals. The pleasant, though unusual, sensations produced in her naked loins beneath her dress signaled that she was feeling the effects of the alcohol. She recognized the sensual sensations, but she was sure that she was in complete possession of her mind and senses. While Clay was pouring her another drink, she tried not to let the image of her husband copulating with Nina Marsdale take shape.

How awful! How could Eddie do this to me? The more she thought about it the more she became aware of the insistent, seething, sensations in her, and thought for a fleeting second that it would serve Eddie right if she were to play at the same game. She soon pushed that thought from her mind. No! I just can't do it! Clay returned to her, handing her the tall glass of scotch. She looked up at him, seeing him for the first time. She saw a stocky, powerfully built man with dark hair, heavy features, and she noted the satisfied leer on his face as he resumed the seat opposite her, lounging back in it to wait. That's it! He's waiting like a cat waiting for a canary! Suddenly Jenna had had enough.

"Mr. Marsdale, I'm not going to have any part of this," she said with determination.

Calmly he said. "It's already been decided. You and I are going to bed and I'm going to fuck you!"

"No!" she gasped. "I won't do it!" "Let's put it another way then. If you don't then your husband will be out of a job and you my dear will lose your lavish lifestyle and be forced like the rest of the women unlucky enough to land a wealthy man to support yourself. Hmmm."

He paused cocking his head to one side as if studying her. "I don't think Ms. Jenna you would care for the nine to five grind and paying your own way through life. Perhaps this is the lesser of two evils?"

"You wouldn't..." Jenna was in full panic. This was blackmail! This was outrageous! How dare he! Oh my God- she would have to get a job! No, no, no!! That wouldn't do. Not for her. She was not destined to be a secretary and frankly with her liberal arts degree and no real skills what the hell else could she do? It never once occurred to Jenna that she was a spoiled, narcissistic little bitch and had she not been so cold to her husband she wouldn't be in this position but naturally in her mind it was all Eddies fault. Eddie that bastard! Marsdale remained as cool as a cucumber.

"Just finish your drink, Jenna. You're going to enjoy this," he said soothingly. His words and the alcohol were beginning to have their effect on the confused wife. She slumped back on the cushions of the couch, sliding down dejectedly, her dress riding up to show the smoothness of her thighs. She didn't care now. She was trapped. Everything seemed hopeless. She was going to pay for Eddie's sins just like some ancient woman from the Bible. The men commit the crimes but the wives always pay. Let him ogle her legs if that's what he wanted. She would not enjoy this but if she had to let him fuck her to avoid getting a job then she would suffer the ten minutes or so it would take him to empty his balls. Plus she could use this as ammunition to ensure Eddie never divorced her! Ha! She would be safe. Eddie under her thumb and her life financially secure. Heaving a huge self indulgent sigh of complete martyrdom she went limp and waited.

Clay waited for a few moments before he reached for her, his hand going out to rest gently on her inner thigh, above the knee, feeling the silky, smooth warmth of her as his hand moved upward, slowly, massaging the creamy flesh until he had reached the hem of her dress; then her legs parted almost imperceptibly, involuntarily, and he moved on upward confidently, the fingers of his hand exploring her searchingly. Now he was up to the pubic hair, unconfined, the blonde down of her softly curling crotch inciting him, inflaming him with hot passion.

Jenna sat, unmoving, except for the involuntary relaxing of her thigh muscles to allow him access to the juncture of her thighs, but she was a mass of rolling sensations. Her body had reacted to him against her will, the sensitive nerve endings, inflamed by the liquor had a mind of their own. She wondered briefly if he had dropped something into her drink. She had heard about something called 'X' on some thriller movie Eddie had watched on Netflix one night but she wasn't paying much attention to it.

Something about the drug being used to drown all inhibitions while heightening sensation making even a nun go wild with need. She dimly realized that whether or not she wanted it, her reasoning mind was no longer in command. Her body was betraying her. She couldn't help herself. His voice came in a fog. "Let's go to your bedroom!" He pulled her, zombie-like, from the sofa and guided her firmly toward the bedroom.

"Get undressed!" he ordered. Trance-like, Jenna turned her back on him and pulled the dress over her head, and then in grim acceptance, she lay down naked on the bed, her legs held tight together, her arms folded over her naked breasts and daring not to look at him.

"Turn over on your stomach!" His voice was getting raspy. Clay Marsdale, still fully clothed, sat down on the bed. Reaching out stubby fingers, he began to trace the outlines of her loveliness, lightly drawing his hand over her back and down across the swelling protuberances of the twin orbs of her smooth-skinned buttocks; then, down over her legs, allowing the fingers to drift up in the inside of her thighs, back to her smooth, white bottom, where he paused to massage and knead, his fingers digging in on the silky skin. His voice was soft, seductive now. "You have a gorgeous body, Jenna."

Then his lips were on her neck, kissing her wetly, his tongue tracing along on down her back, crouching over her as he came to her buttocks, on down her legs to the ankles, back up to the knees, paying special attention to the inside surface of them. His mouth was hot on the outside of her thighs, as he approached the juncture, where he burrowed briefly into the mysterious dark crevice. Finally, after what seemed eons of time to Jenna, he had traversed the full length of her body, down and back up to her neck; then, to her ears, where he inserted the tip of his tongue to tantalize a hole there, running his wet tongue around the rim of it. Jenna shuddered. The slow burning and banked fires in her were partially uncovered, as he had kissed her, and suddenly, she was aware that her body was a raging inferno of fiery sensations, all of which were being generated in her loins. Oh no! It's starting to feel like I'm on fire down there! He's driving me crazy. Oh, God. Help me!

"Turn over!" he commanded. "I want to see whether the front of you is as luscious as the back."

Compliantly, she turned to her back. His tongue darted instantly across the tip of one nipple, his mouth dipping to take the whole aureole in his lips while a hand stroked the other breast, cupping the milk white mound, then kneading it hard, his thumb and forefinger teasing the nipple to painful erectness. Jenna felt the rampaging electricity in her rapidly moistening pussy, and she mewled involuntarily with the pleasurable sensation, knowing that she wanted him. Wanted his cock absorbed into her raging loins. His tongue trailed moistly across her body, stopping momentarily to screw into her navel, then teasingly on downward to the soft blonde curls at the triangle of her belly and thighs. Her legs which she had kept clamped tightly together began involuntarily to relax, her thighs opening slightly to his probing of her private, feminine parts. His tongue was now replaced by his hand. He inserted an exploratory finger into the soft, hair-lined crease, forcing it down, until he found the canopied bud of her clitoris and rubbed his hard finger against it, grunting with satisfaction as it began to grow, blood-engorged, under his titillation of it. Dear God! What's happening to me?

Unexplainably to her, she lost control of her legs. Her thighs suddenly, of their own volition, jerked open wide to him and his head dropped to her cunt, his mouth exploring her until he found the erect, pulsing clitoris in its canopy of slightly darker skin of the fleshy lips of her vulva. She moaned in an agony of pleasure as he found and captured the palpitating button between his teeth and held it lightly, running his tongue in circles around it, decreasing the radius, until at last he released it from his teeth, and his tongue concentrated on the tip of it exclusively.

"Stop it! Please, please, it's driving me crazy!" she moaned in a helpless plea that she knew would not be answered by Clay. The older man opened his mouth wider and moved downward. His tongue slithered into the viscous moistness of her throbbing cunt. With his head buried in the searing muskiness of her pussy, Clay could hear her whimpering mewls each time his tongue swirled around the inside of her velvety, tumescent and softly hair-lined vaginal opening. He drew her legs up and slid his arms under them so that his shoulders and arms were wedged between her now widely opened thighs. In the midst of tongue-fucking her he suddenly realized that within seconds she would be climbing the walls begging him to fuck her. Marsdale then slipped both of his hands underneath her thighs and pushed them up further, allowing her legs to drape over his shoulders. He moved his hands on up to her buttocks, feeling the tiny undulations of them and pulled the cheeks up to him, his stubby fingers digging into her soft flesh.

Jenna cried out her pleasure and frustration as she felt his tongue plunge deeply into the liquid depths of her cunt. She wanted more of it. Instinctively, she reached for the thatch on his head, grasping it, tangling her fingers in the bristly scruff, she tried to pull his head farther into her as the pulsing, and racing sensations of her passion engulfed her. She was helpless in its thrall, and she could but react like a bitch in heat to the sensual sexuality of his probing, searching tongue. She could no longer think. She knew she had to have release from this punishing torment.

"Clay... I've got to have it... now! I want you to put your thing inside me... and do it..." she mumbled, begging him for release from her frustration. Clay raised his head from her cunt to leer down at her lewdly.

"Oh, so you're getting off at last?" he stated.

"Yes... oh, please, do it to me!" she whispered between tightly clenched teeth, her eyes closed to shut out his obscenely ogling face.

"Say it properly, then!" he said quietly. The insanely frustrated young blonde knew what he wanted her to say and she cast aside the Mormon Church to get what she wanted for the first time in her sexual life.

"Fuck me... stick your cock in my cunt... I want your cock fuck me fuck me, Clay... now!"

"Marvelous, you beautiful morsel... now, I want you to help me get my clothes off!" Her words drove his own passion to new heights. His prick jerked and throbbed in the confines of his clothing. He had waited long and patiently while he had teased and tantalized this luscious piece of womanly flesh to advanced sexual need and he knew that she was going to be hot. Jenna came off the bed, leaping to obey him instantly. With trembling fingers she helped him to strip off his clothing, gasping in disbelief as his giant cock was released from the imprisoning shorts.

"No, my God! It's too huge!" she mumbled involuntarily. She knew her own husband was exceptionally big but this man was a sin against nature, he was absolutely gigantic.

"Don't you love it?" he leered.

"I'm afraid... I don't think I can take it all," she said wide-eyed with fear.

"You should learn more about it then. Take it in your mouth and suck it for a while!" Instantly, she balked.

"You must be mad! That's perverted. I won't! I won't!"

"Jesus Christ! You really are right off the farm, aren't you? What quaint little ideas you have about sex. Suck it, baby. Because I'm telling you right now... no suckee... no fuckee! No job for hubby!" He reached for her, running his hands over her breasts, the curve of her waist and thighs, cupping her ass, pulling her loins to his and allowing his thick, lust-filled cock to slip between her thighs, the blood-red cowl of it coming to rest on the clitoral bud as he gently but firmly moved his hips against her in erotic stimulation.

The shock of the shiny, smooth head of his cock on her clitoris was almost more than she could tolerate at this point. She began to move in opposition to him, savoring the surging sensations it caused, moving in wild abandon, her hips gyrating and her moist cunt lips sliding along the length of him. Suddenly he pulled away from her and sat down on the edge of her bed, holding his prick in one hand, he used the other to pull her to a kneeling position between his legs; then he put his strong hand behind her neck and drew her head to his loins, stopping only when her face was scant inches from his massive member.

"Suck me!" he grunted. Reluctantly, she lowered her lips to the blood-engorged tip of it and placed her lips there gingerly, kissing that monstrous cock, doing as he bid, knowing in her mind that it was wrong, but doing it because her body demanded orgasmic release from the sexual torture he had been inflicting upon her. Then, with deep revulsion she took the instrument into her mouth, tasting the pungent maleness of him, surprised at the soft, rubbery texture of the head, as she hollowed her lips in and out, sucking it as he had instructed her.

"Use your tongue!" he commanded. The inexperienced young adulteress touched the head with her tongue and felt the jerking shock of it in him as she swirled her oral member around and around, finally trying to insert the tip of her tongue on the tiny, moistened orifice on the end. His hips began to move, shoving the length of his farther into her mouth. Strangely, now, she began to feel even more sexual excitement, the pounding, crashing, and rhythmic song of desire pulsing through her body demanding its resolution. Then she felt him lie back on the bed, his hands jerking her head upward and away from his ever-growing rod of flesh.

"Now, we'll see how my cock fits in your cunt," he said. Jenna stood up as he moved his heavy body around to lie straight in the bed, on his back, his cock jutting up like a flagstaff.

"Straddle me, my dear," he said, holding out his arms to her, "ride me like a horse." Jenna did not hesitate. She was too ready, far too far along. Instantly, she was atop him, her legs straddling his waist. She grasped his giant pole in her hands and guided it, unerringly to the moist warmth of her hungry cunt. She dropped her weight back on him, absorbing his entire prick within her in one movement, his rock-hard flesh ramming up into her vaginal vault, filling her completely and flicking past the tip of the cervix as it bottomed in her.

Suddenly, he flexed his hips upward, driving his cock even further into her as he felt the silky moistness of her pussy enveloping him with throbbing, searingly hot flesh, and her body squirming above him uncontrollably. She began to move now with wild abandon, rotating her hips and driving her cunt up and down his hardened cock, taking all of him in her velvet-lined cunt with each stroke. She found that by inching her body forward and supporting herself on her hands that she was able to move her hips more freely, and she began furiously to pump her soft, quivering buttocks up and down on him, faster and faster in the inexorable rhythm of love, locked fleshly to him by the erect phallus between them.

The fact that this was a new position for the usually shy inhibited wife did not even faze her. She was too absorbed in the concentration of sensations in her cunt. The freedom to move, to command her own direction and to set her own speed was sheer ecstasy, and she was lost in the morass of never-before-experienced sensations. Bareback and bare assed, Jenna rose him as if she were riding a Brahma bull at a rodeo, taking all of his cock with every jump, unbridled and frantic, fucking him for all she was worth, her hips writhing and pounding against him, rising and falling, swirling in great grinding rotations, her breasts hanging to his chest, the nipples spiking into him, her belly rubbing against his hairy loins, as she leaned further forward. He held the thick length of his prick rigid for her, allowing her to move on him, her wet cunt sliding on his length, out of control. He could not match her beat, so he raised his hips higher, offering up his manhood in sacrifice while she danced the ritual sex dance above him.

He put his clenched fists under his buttocks to raise his cock higher to her thrusting, pummeling cunt. As if going for a blue ribbon, she rode the unbridled, mad bull of a man and it was a never-ending contest, until suddenly she was on the verge of winning the championship. She dashed her mount into it, and she felt it coming at last, a sort of molten lava surrounded and consumed her, the liquid racing through, inside her, and she was at the brink of cataclysmic orgasmic release she strived for which had been denied to her by her newlywed husband. Clay, beneath her, had finally found the rhythm of her headlong ride and rose to meet her churning movements. He thrust up at her, measuring her with his searing rock-hard cock, trying to bury his fleshy shaft deeper into her belly, until they were one in the blazing, flashing inferno of orgasm. Rockets lit up her brain as she felt the whole of her quivering, pent-up being brought to the brink, erupting in her belly like a Roman candle shooting forth its colorful stream of sparks into every part of her salaciously aroused body. His plunging cock brought her well-earned, spewing reward from her wildly panting labors. Beneath her, she heard Clay's harsh cry, frothing forth from his lips, and she could feel the jetting flood of his seminal fluid, sperm-laden, thickly white and viscous, hosing into her from that hardened instrument of lust and pleasure. "Ah! It's almost..."

And with a desperate and final squatting, ramming motion, she forced his spewing prick deeply into her and she was there!

"I'm... ah...At last!" Jenna Harris sat up, his jerking cock still moving in her. She threw her arms high as if she had found true happiness at last. In her dazed sexual reverie she leaned down to Clay and captured his mouth with her own, ramming her tongue into his mouth, savoring the taste of him, and she was supremely happy and at peace with herself. And then she remembered something.

"Does this mean that Eddie won't lose his job," she asked timidly. "We'll see, my dear. It depends on your performance tonight. This afternoon is just the preliminary round. Tonight at my house with your husband will be the real test."

CHAPTER 7

Nina Marsdale received Eddie and Jenna Harris at the door of their magnificent home with grace and tact, not revealing for an instant her wild adultery with Eddie. Her restraint was remarkable. She knew that she would get him into bed again before the night was over. She knew also that her husband, Clay would have Jenna. Where it would go from there was anyone's ballgame. They moved easily into the crowded game room and were served drinks by the bartender that Jenna had seen at Nina's for her afternoon cocktail party. All of the tennis pros and members of the board of directors of Marina Tennis Clinic were there. Eddie, of course, knew all of them but Jenna had a little trouble recognizing some of them out of their usual tennis whites. Jenna soon found herself talking to a buxom brunette with strikingly expressive brown eyes.

"I'm Zelda Watson," the brunette volunteered. "We met briefly the other afternoon at Nina's cocktail party. You're Jenna Harris, aren't you?"

"Yes, Zelda, how are you," she said politely, noting that the older woman was slightly under the influence of alcohol. She was slurring her words but was speaking slowly to make herself understood.

"Nice party," Jenna offered. "I've never been in this part of the house. Is this the game room?" Zelda glugged down the last of her drink and leaned closer to Jenna, lowering her voice, she whispered, "The real games rooms are upstairs in the bedrooms. That's where the most points are scored."

"What games? What do you mean?" Jenna asked naively. A look of startled disbelief crossed Zelda's face. Her voice raised an octave. "Are you kidding? Don't you know? Is this your first party at the Marsdales'?"

"Why yes, except for the other afternoon. Oh, I did have drinks over at Marina one afternoon waiting for Eddie..." Jenna said feeling a little uneasy for the first time.

"Well, babe, you'd better drink up. You're going to need it!"

"Why?" Jenna queried, still not fathoming what the woman was intimating. Zelda moved so close to Jenna that her breath was almost burning her cheek. "When the people from the Marina get together it's not just to talk about tennis. This is a swap party. I thought everyone knew about it. Before the night is over you're going to be fucked and not by your husband. Your husband will be sticking it to someone else. Of course," she added, "You can watch if you prefer that. You get the picture, dearie?"

Jenna didn't answer for several moments her mind a mass of conflicting emotions. Her first impulse was to get up and run out but she was in too deeply now. Now not only was there the problem of Clay's having taped her husband and his own wife but there was now her own adultery as well. Oh why was life so confusing? She was just going to have to stay here and make the best of it.

"You mean to say all of these people here swap?" The slightly drunk brunette nudged her suggestively.

"You got it! They fuck their brains out actually!" Just then a tall, silvery-haired man who was deeply tanned sat down on the other side of Zelda on the upholstered sofa. His quick familiarity with her led Jenna to believe that he must be Mr. Watson but Zelda introduced him as Jeff Mitchell, one of the founders of Marina. As Zelda had turned to talk animatedly with Jeff, Jenna was about to get up to move to another location when Clay Marsdale entered the room. He immediately called for attention.

"I want everyone to have a good time tonight and I'd like to introduce a new couple. Some of you have met them already but anyway here's Eddie and Jenna Harris."

There was a round of applause as he continued, "We hope that they will enjoy their participation in our little get together." Marsdale chuckled along with his guests after that comment. The wealthy man went on, "We have a little entertainment tonight for you. We have some videotape you might enjoy. Lights, Jackie, please..."

Jenna noted just before the lights were extinguished that everyone seemed to be in couples but not with their own spouses. She wondered where Eddie was, but did not see him. She guessed then that he must be with Nina who was not in the room. That meant that she was supposed to be with Clay, she guessed. The Marsdale's must have arranged this, she decided. Clay touched Jenna on the shoulder, then and motioned for her to come sit with him on a seat near the rear of the room so that he could run the equipment.

"Come on, baby," he said as she rose. "I want you beside me." She followed him and sat primly on the seat. Clay sprawled down beside her. He said in a hoarse whisper. "I'm glad you decided to come."

She didn't reply. Instead she turned her attention to the video screen where a tape showing what appeared to be an orgy on a tennis court unfold. Marsdale handed her a drink. She automatically began to sip it, knowing that her reaction to it during the afternoon had been agreeable, and if she must go through with this second sexual encounter with Clay she might as well enjoy it. She really didn't like the man, but she couldn't help remembering that it was he who had given her such a tremendous climax... her first ever. She blushed, recalling the scene vividly, her actions, her words, the sensations that had throbbed through her. Her attention was drawn back to the screen. Suddenly a beautiful brunette flashed on the screen endowed with abundant charms.

When she turns her face toward the camera everyone can see that it is Sally Dunn who works in the pro shop. There are appreciative murmurs from the people in the room. Clay had not touched Jenna up to this point. Now he put his arms around her and fondled a generous breast through her dress. He quickly withdrew his hand. He said, "I hate brassieres. Let's get it off!"

So saying, he took her drink from her hand and

set it aside; then he reached behind and deftly unzipped the back of her dress.

"Stop it. I won't undress in front of all these people," she hissed at him, furious because of the public intimacy.

"Cool it. Hold still. I'll show you in a second what to do," he ordered. Swiftly, he unhooked the snaps in back, pushed the straps of the bra down over her shoulders, then, reaching up into the short sleeves he brought the straps down over her elbows, forearms and hands on each side. Reaching into the top of her dress, he smoothly slipped the lacy bra from her, the straps coming back through the armholes of the dress, the entire garment having been removed through the neck without removing her dress. As much as she hated the thought of being exposed in front of the others still in the room she had to admire the skill with which this man carried off the maneuver.

"Stuff this thing in your bag!" he croaked. Embarrassed, she took the flimsy bra and stuffed it into her handbag. He left the back of her dress unzipped, slipping his hand and arm around her, inside the dress, to a smooth, silken-skinned breast, where he stroked, fondled and kneaded her, the nipple becoming erect under his fingers, the tingling sensation becoming more pleasant with each passing moment. She began to feel light-headed, and guessed that her drink must be the cause of it. The action on the screen again attracted her attention. The man Sally is with is seen to have his hand in Sally's moist crotch, his middle finger stroking her clitoris, her hips moving in opposition to his insistent probing finger. Now the camera returns to Sally's face. She is in the throes of orgasm, her face working, her mouth forming passionate words. She relaxes with the delicious climax and slides from his lap to the floor. The camera plays over her nude body from all angles.

Finally, coming back to the couch where the unknown man lies nude, an enormous, erect penis jutting upward like a stanchion. He beckons to her, then reaches down to take his genitals in his hands. She crawls slithering across the floor to him, reaching the couch, she kneels over his cock, taking it into her hands to fondle it, sliding the foreskin back, reaching under to knead his testicles, and showing with a two-hand hold the tremendous length of him. Now Sally kisses the end of his prick and takes it into her mouth, her cheeks hollowing in and out as she begins to suck on it. Slowly, she begins to slide her mouth up and down, her head bobbing, as with each down stroke she takes more and more of his lengthy tool into her mouth. The camera cuts to Sally's young face, and then divulges her ecstasy at the lewd behavior. Jenna felt suddenly ill as revulsion overcame her. She tried to free herself from Marsdale's grasp. She was very angry.

"I'm not going to watch this disgusting exhibition."

Clay was quite calm. "Would you rather watch your husband's performance on the screen, then? We get around to all of us at one time or another. We like to be stars in our little galaxy here."

"You bastard!" she spat out. Unperturbed, his mouth captured hers, his tongue invading her lashing through the barrier of her teeth. He bore her backward until she was prone on the bench, his hand going under her skirt to caress her warm, smooth thighs, coming, finally to the softly curling genital mound. There he pulled down the front of her sheer panties and insinuated a finger into her moist, open slit. He found her tiny, enshrined clitoris and moved his finger on it, bringing the bud of her womanhood to erection.

"No Clay. Not here, please!" she gasped.

"Look around, sweetheart," he said. "Over there on the couch it would appear that Zelda is enjoying Jeff Mitchell to the fullest." Jenna looked toward the couch. She saw Zelda leaning over the sprawling form of the older man. His zipper was undone and she had his long cock in her mouth, her head bobbing slowly up and down, her cheeks hollowing in and out as he sucked on the rigid, erectness of him.

"Dear Lord!" she exclaimed and averted her eyes. "And over there, in the corner is Jeff's wife with Dave Carlson. He seems to be fucking her in the ass on the floor. Our only black tennis pro is eating out..."

"Stop it!" she hissed. She closed her eyes, covering them with her hands, trying to blot out the images she saw. It was too much for her... too depraved... filthy... perverted.

"I thought Marina was an exclusive club. I never realized these people were like animals..."

"Come on. You haven't seen anything. Upstairs in the bedrooms there's probably six or seven couples indulging themselves," he said matter-of-factly. All during this time, Clay had stroked her clitoris affectionately, with feather like strokes of his fingers, and she began to move her buttocks in small circles against his hand, unable to control her urge to do so. The building up of the delicious sensations slashed at her, converging on that spot where his finger insistently rubbed and titillated her. Jenna had not seen her husband for some time. Actually, soon after their arrival, he had seemed to disappear. She opened her eyes and looked about the dim room carefully.

None of the men present seemed to resemble him in any way. She had some difficulty in recognizing anyone at all; almost every person in the room was engaged in some form of sexual activity. Clay stood up.

"I think it's time for you and I to go upstairs to really do things right." He zipped up the back of her dress and pulled her to her feet. She rose reluctantly, his strong grip of her hand reminding her how badly he wanted her. She moved with him, leaving the screening room, unnoticed by any of the copulating couples. Together, they mounted the broad staircase to the second floor. Jenna's stomach fluttered with fear and a certain, strange anticipation that she could not define. Checking at the various bedroom doors one by one, Marsdale ascertained that all of the bedrooms were filled with one or more couples and a few trios. Words and phrases drifted out to them along the unmistakable sounds of wild uninhibited fucking.

"Come into my study," he said. "I want to show you some pictures." They stepped into the masculine appointed study. She gasped. On the walls were pictures of couples in lewd poses. She recognized many of the people in the pictures. Most of them were in this house now, engaged in illicit sex. The photos turned her stomach. They were explicit in detail and no depravity had escaped Clay's camera. Then, a completely inexplicable thing occurred in the young wife. The drinks, the digital stimulation of her breasts and clitoris, the lewd videotape, the salacious pictures on the wall, the knowledge that this man wanted her sexually, and her own need all combined suddenly to give her the most erotic and sudden urge she had ever experienced. She felt the moistness between her legs, the keening sensations that coiled and recoiled inside her, striking her there violently, surging out along her nerve endings only to return throbbing, to her innermost womanly parts, and she knew that she was becoming more and more ready for anything.

She noticed the bulge in Marsdale's trousers, and she knew that he, too, was more than ready; however, she averted her eyes, not daring to look, to admit to herself that she could possibly be interested in his sexual organs. He came to her and put his arms around her, slipping his hands down to cup her buttocks and pull her flaming loins close in to him, grinding his hard penis into her.

"I want to show you one last thing," he said. Reaching over and behind her, he snapped out the lights and pushed aside his books on a bookshelf, revealing a lighted bedroom beyond a glass mirror.

"It's a one-way mirror," he enlightened. Jenna's eyes were riveted on the bed. She couldn't help watching, now, as she gazed with increasing interest and curiosity, trying to make out details in the softly lighted room. Her view was from the foot of the bed, and she could see that there was a man and woman on the bed, their limbs intertwined, the man above, the woman on her back, her legs flexed upward and drawn back toward her chest. She could see the thick cock inserted, deeply, in the woman's glistening, wet cunt, spreading the soft folds of her furrow, the brown, round anus, darkly, below, the balls of the man hanging down from between muscular and hairy legs. The man withdrew, slowly, until she could see, clearly, the underside of the glans. Then, he plunged the monstrous prick straight into the small woman and she imagined that she could hear the slap of their pelvises as the thick, rock-hard rod of flesh went in, burying its length completely in the soft, female flesh. The young wife was now aware that Clay was grinding his pelvis into her loins, his cock sticking out from his trousers, as he tried to shove it between her legs, and unconsciously, she found herself responding to his obscene caress, sliding her pelvis up and down on him through the rough cloth of his trousers. "Do you want to hear what they're saying?" he asked.

He reached up beside the books again and snapped a switch, not waiting for her to make up her mind. A speaker inside the bookshelf amplified the sound of the low voices from the bedroom.

"Oh, Eddie," the woman said. "Fill my cunt with your cock... mmm... it's so big... so hard..." Jenna gasped, reddening and turned her head away from the lewd spectacle.

"Is that my husband?" she asked, weakly sagging in his arms, "with your wife?" Marsdale held her tight.

"Let's wait and see."

Now the man's voice was heard. "Nina, baby... I fit so well in you... your cunt is so juicy... I love my cock inside you..."

Marsdale reached behind her and snapped the lights back on in his study. Instantly, the scene in the adjoining bedroom was blotted out, and she realized that one of the properties of a one-way mirror was that the viewer be in semi-darkness. Reaching up behind her, Clay gripped the zipper of her dress and pulled, down smoothly. Then, grasping the hem of her dress he began to pull the garment over her head.

"Not here..." she gasped.

"Why not. It's just as good a place as any," he said. He flung her dress to the back of a chair, reached for her and clamped wet lips to a puckering, pink nipple, taking the whole areola into his mouth and sucking on it, using his teeth to nip at the rapidly hardening flesh. Then, he paid tribute to its mate, as he kneaded her soft, mounding femaleness in his rough hands. Now, he slid his hands behind her, slipping one hand inside her panties to fondle and knead her smooth, round buttocks; then, with a deft movement he stripped the thin, nylon garment down over her tapering thighs to her trim ankles. Jenna stepped out of her shoes and he stooped down to remove the sheer underclothing from her feet, sailing it across the room to join her dress. She was now completely nude before him, stripped of all her barriers. Instantly, his finger began taunting her sensitive clitoris, and Jenna gasped with the ecstasy of it, in spite of herself.

Her body was beginning to feel, blazingly, on fire, a fire that could not be extinguished, a fire that threatened to consume her and she could do nothing. Stepping back from her, Marsdale began to remove his own clothing, deliberately, methodically. Soon, he too was naked, his enormous cock standing out thick and long before him, blood-engorged and throbbing with the passion of his need for her. Jenna stared. She was horror stricken. The size of him was mammoth. She couldn't believe her eyes, yet she knew that he had rammed that giant hunk of meat into her little cunt this very afternoon. She had taken all of it into her and had loved every minute of it!

"Here, dear, I'll put a blanket on my desk," he said when suddenly a familiar sing-song voice came into the room over the amplifier.

"Shove your fingers in my asshole! Make me cum, Eddie!" Jenna turned to Nina's husband, pleadingly. "

Turn it off. I can't bear listening to that."

"But my dear it's wonderfully erotic. Nina is a fabulous woman in the sack. She just loves to get fucked in the ass," he said nonchalantly as though he was talking about her love of French cuisine or foreign films.

"Lie down on my desk top!" he ordered. Jenna complied sick at heart a complete feeling of hopelessness in her. Eddie's boss clambered to the desk top, placing himself over her, in reverse, with his thick, hardened prick over her face, his legs spread on either side of her head. Leaning down on his hands and knees, he said,

"Take all of my cock in your mouth and suck me off! Suck hard and lick me! You can use your teeth but be careful!"

Jenna reached up to him, taking his thick, awesome instrument in her hands sliding the slack foreskin back to reveal the blood-red hooded cowl of his penis and took in into her mouth, tasting the male taste of him and inwardly appalled with the realization of what she was doing. Experimentally, she began to suck, using her tongue to lave the giant head of him filling her mouth, swirling her lingual member around and around it, trying, finally, to insert the tip of her tongue into the tiny slit in the tip of the glans. Marsdale leaned forward and down into the sixty-nine position and with a groan, buried his lips in her thoroughly moistened cunt. His tongue lashed out and probed wetly at her downy hair-lined vaginal opening, then moved up to the clitoral bud, licking her to a higher pulsing excitement than she had ever before experienced. Against the orders of her reasoning mind, her body reacted, and she began to move her hips up to him, rhythmically, her pink-lined pussy on fire, begging for more of that sensuous tongue.

Oh God. Believe me. I don't want this. But, I can't seem to help myself. The sounds of the lovemaking from the next room came to them through the amplifier; the sounds of slapping flesh and punished bed springs, the squeaks and heavy breathing becoming louder and more rapid, building to an orchestral climax. Nina was screaming out orders.

"Faster, Eddie... harder... fuck me harder... I'm almost there... oh your cock is stuffing me so full. I'm there... oh fuck... fuck me... fuck me... I'm coming!" The squeaking went on, faster and faster, then, suddenly stopped, and followed by wetly slapping sounds, accompanied by squeals from the bed.

Eddie's voice was hoarse and muffled. "Oh you fabulous cunt... I'm going to come too... I'm shooting all my jizz in you... oh, it's wonderful... here I go..." Jenna was sickened by the explicit sounds of sex from the bedroom. Eddie was spewing his hot sperm into another woman, but somehow, the sounds of it and knowledge worked to increase the delicious sensations in her own loins, the generated heat in her forcing her to jerk her crotch upward, her legs splayed out, to the insistent mouth of Clay Marsdale, and she moaned out her helpless need of the older man.

"God, Clay, I want it too. I want you to fuck me," she gasped completely out of breath. The older man raised his dripping face, sex-juices mingled with sweat from her overly moistened cunt. He crawled backward from her, allowing her freedom to move on the desk top. He kneeled up on his knees and leered down at her.

"Get up on your hands and knees! I'm going to fuck you in the ass!" She cringed away from him, whimpering.

"No! Oh, God. You'll kill me! I'm a virgin there!" She jumped off the desk. Marsdale jumped down from his desk to stand before her. His huge cock had begun to soften, slightly. He took it in his hands and said.

"Before I can ram this right up your tiny little asshole you'll have to get it good and hard again." In a trance, she knelt before him; taking his giant phallus into her hands and working the slack skin back and forth several times, feeling it begin to grow in her hands. She took it gently, in her mouth and began to suck like a demon not knowing why she did so. In a few moments his rod returned to its former degree of hardness. He moved his hips back, suddenly, pulling the hard flesh of him from her lips. She tried to recapture it. He shoved her back on her heels and restrained her with his hands on her shoulders.

"Okay," he gasped. "Now get up and lean forward... all the way forward with your tits on the desk!" Reluctantly she did as she was bade. He came to her and reached down to the protruding, smoothly rounded and defenseless buttocks. With a middle finger, he probed the soft, white crease until he found the puckered, brown ring of her anus, as his other hand drew a cheek of her ass aside. His probing finger found it and he worked the tip of the digit into the opening up to the first knuckle, then, with a constant pressure, he shoved in all the way.

"Nooo... nooo... stop!" she moaned.

"Be still now. I put something on your little bung hole to ease it for you but if you fight it will hurt that much more."

Ignoring her protests, he worked his finger around in the sponginess of her back channel, until he felt the sphincter muscle begin to relax. Now, he withdrew the finger and replaced it with two, repeating the process of stretching her small, tight anal opening; then, yet a third time he reamed her, using three fingers.

"Okay, baby, you're ready... let's get a cock up your ass!" Reaching under her, he dipped his fingers in her cunt, moist and ready, using the wetness to lubricate his great cock. With the thumbs of both hands he spread the cheeks of her ass exposing the round anal ring, little edges of the pink, inner flesh showing; then, he placed the head of his shaft, blood-engorged and throbbing, against the defenseless opening. He pushed. The head of his prick entered her, surging past the tight, elastic ring of muscles. He stopped when she cried out.

"Stop it! You're splitting me in half!" she shrieked. He expanded the head of his cock several times; each time bringing moans of pain from her, until finally, with a powerful flick of his hips he shoved into her, all the way, driving into the spongy tissue of her back passage, expanding it and pulling the brown edges inside, as the massive pole skewered her. Now, with his full length and thickness buried in her, he paused again, waiting for her anal canal to adjust.

"It's like having a cannon back there. Stop it. Take it out, Clay!" she demanded. Marsdale stood behind her, leaning back, slightly, and began to move his hips, slowly, at first, grinding into her with short strokes, feeling the clasping, anal muscles constrict against him, now, increasing gradually, to longer and longer strokes, rhythmically, fucking into her tight little asshole, the sensations coming to him stronger and stronger with every stroke into her.

"Fuck back against me!" he grunted. Experimentally, Jenna moved her hips back, in opposition to him. She found to her surprise that it was not as uncomfortable now. Her whole pelvic region was aflame. Her moist, now ready cunt cried for fulfillment, too. She wanted to be filled and fucked everywhere, at the same time. She began to waggle her hips with abandon and sureness back up in the air, the pleasurable sensations mixed with her perverse nature and something in her demanded more and more. What's happening to me, she wondered? This is the worst sin against nature and I want more of it.

"Clay! I want more! I want something shoved in my cunt too!" she wailed, amazingly.

"I don't have a vibrator here. Wait a minute, though," he said with a lewd leer appearing on his sweating countenance. Still fucking into her he leaned across the desk of his study and took something off the wall. It was the racquet that had won him the

Pacific Coast Tennis Tournament some twenty years earlier.

"Use this!" She had no idea of what he was talking about. "What do you mean?" she asked, confusion running rampant in her tortured mind.

"Use the racquet handle to fuck yourself with," he said. Knowing that she couldn't help herself, the demands of her body slashing at her brain, she reacted wildly to fill the great need in her. She reached back and under with the old style wooden racquet, and began rubbing the leather grip over the canopied bud of her womanhood. Greedily, hungrily, she stroked the handle up and down on the miniature phallus. The streaking, electric charge in her nerves was more than she could stand. She withdrew her hand only to put it back instinctively, inserting the leather grip handle into the moist void of her vagina. Tentatively she tried pushing the hard wooden handle just inside the mouth of her cunt. She began to saw the racquet handle in and out, in rhythm with Clay, waggling her hips back and forth, reveling in the keening sensation of having both cunt and asshole filled. In and out, ceaselessly she perversely fucked herself while Clay Marsdale sodomized her from behind with the merciless abandon of a wild buffalo. Meanwhile, next door, in the bedroom, Jenna's husband had spewed his sperm far up into Nina Marsdale's hungry, demanding cunt, grunting out his sexual satisfaction and collapsing atop her. He had brought the Oriental woman to climax three times. She, even, was spent for the time being.

A few minutes later, she wanted a cigarette and a drink. Dutifully, Eddie rolled off the Marsdale's bed and went to get the cigarettes from the dresser and the drinks from the bureau. Glancing into the mirror on the wall at the foot of the bed, he saw his own still jutting reflection, but there was something more; he saw shadowy motion that was not being reflected from the bedroom. He was certain that he and Nina were alone in the room. Puzzled, he brought the drinks and lighted cigarettes to the bed. As he passed the mirror, again, he realized that she was seeing into another room and... That's it... it's a one-way mirror! He went to the wall switch near the door and snapped the lights off. Nina watched him with amusement, a sly smile complacently playing on her lips.

"Why'd you do that?" she asked.

"I want to know what's going on with that mirror," Eddie said. He stood before the mirror and saw into what he recognized as a kind of study. In profile view, he suddenly saw in horrified recognition, his young newlywed wife, Jenna, completely naked, bending over a desk and Clay Marsdale slaving away behind her, moving his hips back and forth, shoving his monstrously erect cock into his wife's asshole! He was stunned beyond belief!

"It's Jenna and Clay! Your husband is fucking my wife in the ass!" he roared, bounding nakedly, for the door. His hand was on the door knob jerking open the door when Clay's Chinese wife's voice stopped him.

"Hold it, Eddie. It isn't what you think! Jenna is fucking Clay because she wants to!" she said with conviction. She came off the bed with feline grace.

"Would you like to hear what's going on in there," she asked, smiling her inscrutable little smile. Reaching out to the side of the mirror, she pressed a button. Instantly, the bedroom was flooded with the lewd, amplified sounds from her husband's study. Jenna's voice came to them unmistakable from the speakers.

"Clay! I want more! I want something shoved in my cunt too!"

Eddie froze! Jesus, suffering Christ! She's asking for it! Things began to form together in his mind.

"Did he show Jenna the videotape of me with Sally Dunn? Is that why she's doing this? Did you trap both of us?"

"Really Eddie, are you trying for an academic award or something? Stop being so Goddam melodramatic! It's just a little device we use to get couples to swap. A little subtle persuasion, shall we say?"

"More like blackmail," he grunted.

"That is a little harsh, Eddie. You're a big boy now. You can make up your mind about things. All the others at the club have."

"But my wife... it's not right!"

"Oh, I see. The old double standard rears its ugly head. She has every right to enjoy sex and get the most out of it."

She reached down between them to fondle his flaccid prick. It was beginning to grow harder in her hand. Suddenly, he had an idea that came to him in his anger. He had been asking himself questions, but there had been precious few answers coming to him from the welter of conflicting thoughts. Now, the one idea was foremost in his mind. He put his distorted, single-track idea into immediate use, not thinking, not considering the rightness of it, nor the wrongness of his actions.

"Come on, Nina," he said. "Let's make this a real

party! Let's go into the study!"

Nina smiled up at him, her brown Oriental eyes shining, "I thought you'd never get around to it," she said. Then, more loudly, "Clay darling. We're going to join you!"

Marsdale's voice came over the speaker to them. "By all means my love," he grunted, as he ground himself harder into Eddie's wife's tight little asshole. Nina and Eddie came into the study. Jenna was only partially aware that they were there. She was absorbed, mesmerized. She continued to try and cram the tennis racquet handle full length into her cunt but of course it was impossible.

Eddie was sickened, but he would not change his mind now. He took charge of the scene.

"Get her on the desk! I'm going to fuck her cunt at the same time, I've always wondered what double-penetration would feel like," he said. Marsdale glanced up at him, pleased with his employee's inventiveness.

Together, they maneuvered Jenna, who was only half-conscious of what was going on, to the desk top. Clay took her again, burying his thick cock deeper up her ass and rolling to his back with Jenna impaled like a fly on top of him. Her cheating husband clambered to the desk top and planted himself astraddle of Marsdale's legs, spread his wife's thighs and pushed the tennis racquet aside and aimed his massive cudgel at her warmly dripping cunt and rammed it home in her vaginal vault. "Is that enough cock for you now?" he screamed pumping furiously. Jenna screamed with the realization of what he was doing.

"Have you gone mad? Ohhhhh!" she cried in uncontrollable ecstasy. Blindly, he fucked into her, his passion mounting. As he plunged, wildly, into the softness of her open, flowering cunt, he could feel the huge bulge of Marsdale's cock through the thin wall of tissue separating her vagina and anal passage. Jenna was shocked, almost horrified beyond reason when Eddie mounted her and thrust into her with such violence, but strangely, unaccountable, the two massive pricks ravishing both pelvic orifices began to bring her to an unknown ecstasy. She was beginning to feel completely filled and fulfilled. The delirious transport glazed her eyes, and she was half-unconscious, aware only of the slamming sensations in her loins. She could not move. Could not react. She was skewered on two giant all-consuming cocks. All she could do was lie there and let the two men ram their monstrous shafts into her; however, she could not understand why her husband had joined them. Oh, Eddie, what's happening to us?

Nina could stand it no longer. She had to have a piece of the action. She climbed to the top of the desk and insinuated her lithe Oriental body between Eddie and Jenna, her crotch over Jenna's face. Jenna had never done it before, but suddenly, she knew what she must do. Her tongue snaked out and began to lick and probe, tasting the femaleness of her, as well as the pungent cum that Eddie had left there, deep in the vaginal vault of Nina Marsdale. Clay, beneath her, reached his climax. He grunted his satisfaction, as his cock jetted white, hot streams of viscous sperm into her back passage. Her jerked upward, spasmodically, driving deeper and deeper into her backside; finally, he dropped back spent, his cock jerking until the full load of sperm had been expended, deep, deep in the far hidden recesses of the young, lust-crazed wife's asshole. Eddie was like a machine, as he pistoned into Jenna, and now she was on the brink of orgasmic release. She felt it coming. Her body thrashed about, deliciously, the sensations shaking her, slicing into her and leaving her satiated, spent, on the verge of unconsciousness. Dimly, as in a dream, she heard her own scream, a piercingly high note ricocheting through the room. "Oh you bastards! Fuck me! Fuck every hole! Aaah... oh... in my cunt... in my ass... fuck me... fuck me... harder... harder... faster... I'm almost... oh... there... I'm... coming!" Jenna had turned her face aside as she came to her release.

Nina atop her realized that she could not function for her, now. Glancing down between her legs, she saw that Jenna's eyes were closed now that she was practically unconscious.

"Fuck me now, Eddie!" Nina said, desperately, sliding back and raising her hips to him. Eddie knelt up and slid his cock rigidly into her moistly ready cunt in one smooth motion, ramming the shaft all the way home in her. He was a wild man. He fucked with driving fury. He machine gunned into her as she demanded. Nina responded to him with like abandon. She came back at him with strong, vigorous strokes of her own, and the massive hardness of him filled her and brought her to the heights. She came and came again, her orgasm bringing with it a euphoria and completeness, and her cry of joy resounded, again and again, but she could not relax, yet. Eddie was still driving into her, his own ejaculation delayed. She knew that she would have to help bring him to release.

"Would it be easier for you to come if you do what we did the other night?" she asked. "

Christ, yes!" he gasped under his mighty laboring. Reaching back and under, Nina guided his giant phallus, alternating between her softly pliant cunt and the resilient sponginess of her voraciously sucking asshole. In a few strokes... asshole... cunt... asshole... cunt... his sperm shot into her vaginal vault, hosing through him, pumping with unrelenting force, the viscous semen spewing in an almost endless stream. Now,

Eddie collapsed on top of Nina, and the mass of tangled bodies was quiet, sexually satiated for the time being. The only sound was the sound of labored breathing. Later in the early hours of the morning back in the comfort of the Marsdale's bedroom there was a more leisurely sex-game and a straight-forward explanation and detailed discussion of the Marsdale's swapping parties. Eddie listened to the explanation of Clay's videotaping and about how that was his usual modus operandi. The young husband couldn't be too angry. He had brought his wife to new heights of sexual abandon that may never have occurred otherwise. Jenna too was happy that it had happened. She couldn't wait to try other members in the club. There was that huge black man she had seen downstairs with that giant black cock... Two more happy converts to swapping lay in the big bed with the Marsdale's eager to try out still more innovations. Yes it had been blackmail but my God it had been worth it!

THE END

AUTHOR LINKS & FREE EXCERPTS

If you enjoyed this please see the author page for a complete listing of books and short stories at the following links. Please do feel free to leave a review and enjoy the free excerpts below. Thanks for reading!

https://www.goodreads.com/author/show/2868139.Catherine_Rose

Follow on twitter for spam free updates on new free releases (short stories) and published novels.
https://twitter.com/adarklydreaming

Excerpt from **'The Castaway's'** now available at most e-book retailers. Just look for
ISBN: 9781311275042

"You know you want it," she said, hotly. She was right. I hadn't even rubbed my button since we'd gotten here. It was kind of hard to find any privacy in a little hut stuffed with five other girls. She ran her tongue across my nipples, and then slurped them into her mouth, suckling lightly, bringing them erect. My breasts swelled and hardened as her hands and mouth worked on them, and I started to drift off into a pleasurable daze.

She slid down my body, her tongue licking wide trails across my chest, and stomach, and abdomen. Then she was between my legs and twirling that wonderful tongue in and out of my slit. Her fingers rubbed back and forth across my clitty, sending me into groaning, grunting spasms of ecstasy, making me come with a devastating fury. She scurried around on her knees, her tongue and mouth latched onto my slit. Her groin moved around over my face, and then slowly lowered. I looked up at her bare crotch, and as if in a dream, watched it approaching me. Then my hands slid up around her buttocks, feeling and remembering the wonderful softness of her skin as I drew her closer. My tongue slid up and down along her slit, making her shiver atop me. She lay fully over me, her breasts in my belly and mine in hers. I could feel the hard little points of her nipples against my skin as she worked on my clit once more. I opened my mouth wide and engulfed almost her entire pubic mound, munching lightly. Then I moved my lips against her hot button and sucked it into my mouth, humming and buzzing to set the little bud vibrating.

I heard Grace moan from down between my legs, and the sound sent a surge of lust through me. I renewed my effort, driving my tongue deep into her slit, gulping down girl juice, rasping my nose, and lips and tongue across her clit. Her body shuddered all over, and her fingers stabbed deep into my cunt as she came. I kept working fiercely on her engorged love nubbin until she finished her orgasm, then went back to a more leisurely licking and sucking. I slid my hands back and forth over her thin buttocks, and then down along her sides to her breasts. I pushed my hands between us and squeezed her breasts, searching for the nipples.

Suddenly I became aware of a pair of bare feet and legs standing inches from my head. I gasped and shoved Grace, dumping her off sideways, and bolting upright, arms crossed over my breasts, and hand over my pussy. Grace looked around in confusion and her eyes opened in shock. She too covered herself. I turned to find three boys grinning there beside us. Their faces were leering and nasty as they beheld us. "Looks like we found a couple of dykes," one said.

"Maybe she needs a spanking," Andrea purred, raising her eyes at Peter.

"Maybe she does," he grinned. I started backing up, my hand dragging Grace with me, but I banged into something, actually someone. It was another boy behind us. He grabbed me, throwing his arms around me, pinning my arms to my sides. There was a second boy there, and he shoved Grace forward so hard, she fell to her knees.

"What a bad little girl," Andrea said, mockingly. Peter grabbed her and dragged her up by her hair, then Tad moved forward and grabbed the waistband of Grace's pants and jerked them down off her flailing legs, leaving her naked from the waist down. Then he ripped open her shirt, and he and Peter worked it off her, leaving her nude. Andrea watched Grace struggling with a cool detached amusement, her eyes sparkling with every grunt or curse Grace made.

"Filthy language for a little girl to use," she cooed. Peter knelt and bent Grace across his knee, so her ass was facing Andrea and Cathy. Grace's entire body was flushed red with fury and humiliation as

Peter brought his hand up and then swung it down against her buttocks with a loud crack.

Grace gasped, but kept her teeth gritted together, determined not to give Andrea the satisfaction of hearing her cry out. Peter was undeterred. He brought his hand up again and then swung down once more, and then again, and again, and again. I struggled uselessly against the boy holding me as Peter spanked his big hand down against Grace's ass cheek over and over. Her ass turned a deep shade of red as he smacked her. I could see Andrea's smile deepening. Grace's ass cheeks were a flaming red, and each time Peter's hand came down it left a white handprint, that quickly faded to red.

Excerpt from '**The Dark Side**'.

ISBN: 9781311698315

"What's this?" I asked him.
He smiled.
"Drink it," he said to me.
I wasn't sure I wanted to. I mean, I had no real reason not to. Even though my hands were tied, I could still move them in front of me. I just felt a little uneasy, the slightest bit of apprehension starting to tighten my stomach. I glanced down at my bound hands and flexed my fingers trying to find a way to make this alright in some way that would ease the growing apprehension I felt.

"I, I think-"
The words stammered out with an uneasy breath and he interrupted before I could even verbalize the

words to express my fears.

"I said drink it."

He didn't sound menacing or anything like that but rather his tone seemed to be the slightest bit more forceful the second time around.

It was enough for me. I could freak and scream while running for the door or I could play this thing out. I didn't argue any further. If he wanted me to drink the damn stuff, then I would. I was going let him think I was doing it to please him and let him think I was being a good little girl but the reality was I had a 'fuck you' attitude that would be damned before I let him see I was actually a bit scared.

No problem. So I took the drink, and downed it. Swiftly, too swiftly I would realize later. Perhaps if I'd taken more time, I might have realized that there was a slightly funny taste to the liquid that left a sweet soft aftertaste on my tongue that I couldn't identify.

I didn't about it until it was too late as was my habit more often than not. But I couldn't stop rolling my tongue against the roof of my mouth wondering if this time I had truly fucked up. And then, it was just that; too late to turn back. Too late for regrets or kicking myself for being such a dumbass. My hands went to my head as I felt a warm fuzzy sensation infuse my body and muddle away any sense of unease I had. An overwhelming sense of calm pervaded and left me standing there with a goofy grin on my face.

"What's the matter?""

I licked my lips and noticed a strange light in his eyes as he watched me.

"I don't know. I feel dizzy.odd and in a way I've never felt before. It's a bit unnerving."

"Well. Don't worry."

He walked towards me and stood so close if I took a deep breath my breasts would mash into his chest. I had a brief image of his flashing teeth as he grinned at me, then through a tunnel I heard his voice fading away.

"Not to worry Clare everything will be just as you ever dreamed it could be and then…."

And then the world went black. When I awoke, I was. Well, let me see if I can describe this scene to you. I was standing on my feet, stripped of my clothes. I had no idea how they had gotten off me. Of course, I knew, but I didn't really want to know. So I pretended it was a mystery. My arms were suspended well above my head hanging by ropes that were entwined around my wrists. And that hurt. Kind of a dull ache that kept my attention.

Now, as I looked down, I saw my feet spread on the floor, attached to cuffs that were held in place by short, strong chains. I sensed something else was off- raising my head I squinted my eyes and tried to remember exactly what my impressions were on first entering this room and finally I got it. The lighting was different. It was all glowing and wonderful and oh so damn creepy. At that moment I wished I could erase every horror movie I had ever watched from my memory. Just scrub it clean because with my vivid and overactive imagination I was quickly panicking and thinking just maybe the driver was going to be the one to dispose of my corpse after play time was over.

I squeezed my eyes shut and did the deep breathing that was going to signal me to stop this weird dream. Ok. Wake up! Open your eyes and you will be in your room. All back to normal. I winked open one eye and saw enough to realize this was no dream. Giving up I opened the other eye and rattled my chains in sheer frustration. Stupid- stupid-stupid, fucking idiot! Now what? No fancy moves here dummy. I heaved a sigh and looked up at my hands. I couldn't see any way to get myself free of the restraints. My mind just went blank. I couldn't even form a coherent thought on how I might get myself out of this one.

After a good ten minutes of freak out which involved nothing more than pulling on the bindings that kept my arms pulled above my head leaving me no wiggle room I gave up and decided to see what I could see by examining my surroundings.

Peering around did nothing to ease the panic that gripped me. I was not in a space decorated by a devotee of Martha Stewart Living that was for damn sure. The lightening was a bit stronger than when I first arrived and now it showed me for the first time just what this room look like. A dungeon! That's where I was! Oh well this was just lovely I went out for drink and now I was locked inside of a dungeon, with a gorgeous hunk of a man who somehow got off on having me naked, in chains. Well, not completely naked. He did have the courtesy, or the good sense, or the what-have-you to leave my garter belt and stockings on. Maybe he was just another bored good looking asshole that had read one of those 'Fifty Shades' of something books and decided to make himself into a role playing hero of kink. Well at least that was what I was hoping for at this point because the alternative was unthinkable.

Leaving me like this; nearly naked and trussed like a gift well I had no doubt that was a big turn-on for him. Otherwise why do it? Maybe I could play his game. Hell I had no choice. I had to play if I wanted to walk out of here.

I could tell by the fact that he had left me with just my stockings, shoes and garters it was purposeful and had to mean something. I took stock of what I must look like to one that would be appraising me like a fine horse for sale.

And there was nothing I could do about it. Nothing! I was embarrassed, to say the least. My lovely, natural full tits, which I took pride in, and which I showed off only to men whom I deemed fortunate and deserving enough to see them, were glistening with my own sweat and standing at sweet attention. Oh, he was a stickler for detail, and he knew that with my arms overhead, my tits would have to stand perkily thrust out for him.

"Well," he said, grinning."

Shit. I hadn't heard him in the room. I wondered if he had been behind me watching me struggle and rail against the chains in sheer frustration.

"You look beautiful."

I didn't say anything. I had no idea what I could say! I stared at him. Now, he was out of his good-looking tailored suit, and wearing something else. A kind of leather jock strap, with studs around his balls and a leather shaft that seemed custom-designed to fit his cock. In other words, his prick and balls were sheathed, outlined in leather. And his left nothing to the imagination, I bit my lip in an effort not to laugh. My first reaction was that he looked ridiculous my next was holy shit he had some cock! Enormous! And he was wielding it with a mighty, macho swagger. Every time he moved, his shaft swung a little. And I couldn't take my eyes off of it!

"What's the matter," he said to me, smiling." Don't you like the way it looks?"

I made no reply; it just seemed safer to keep my mouth shut.

"Come on. Tell me."

Ok well then he obviously wanted a positive response and I had to admit I liked the idea of a massive cock.

"I like it," I said, blushing.

"Good."

"Why am I- why did you?"

"Tie you up and hang you on your wrists? I figured I'd do something to you you'd never forget."

Ok- this was good. If he didn't want me to ever forget than perhaps my imminent death was not part of the night's festivities after all. I relaxed just slightly with a sense of hope but also feeling a slight warming in my lady bits. God I am so pathetic. Trussed up like a turkey by what could be an honest to God head case and I'm getting turned on.

"So what exactly is the plan?"

He came up close to me, and put his handsome face near to mine. And then he explained what the itinerary was.

"I'm going to whip you."

That was it. The whole kit and caboodle!

"What?"Disbelief evident in my voice.

"I said I'm going to whip you," he grinned like it was Christmas.

"No. please. Don't." I pleaded because it seemed like the smart response and frankly I had no desire to have my flesh left with welts from some leather strap. But my pleas fell on predictably deaf ears. There was nothing I could say or do that was going to make any sort of difference with this man. He had it in his mind that he wanted to use a whip on me. On me! I'd never so much as been bruised by a man. Granted Tim had spanked me that time but I don't think he left dark marks on my abused flesh. This guy in front of me? I had an idea that he would leave scars if I wasn't careful how I played this.

And now just because I had been careless I was in the clutches of one that was, to say the least, a little on the wacky side. But, what can I say? I don't want to mislead you. It was turning me on! It was getting to me. And he knew it the bastard!

I guess that's why he continued to grin, even as he went to his wall and plucked off a short, nasty little black whip. He brought it over to me and bent it slightly in front of my face.

"This is my punisher," he said, softly. "I use it on women when they need to be punished. When they need to be taught a lesson."

"But. I haven't done anything."

"You, missy, are a ball-breaker. I can see it all over your face. In the way you smile, in the clothes you wear. You tease men, and I don't like that. You have to be broken. And I'm going to be the one to break you."

What, the fuck? Break me? Ok now I was getting more freaked out and losing the idea that this might be hot.

"Please. Don't."

"Oh, you can beg, all right. You can beg all you want, but it won't do you a bit of good. And I'll tell you something else. By the time I'm through with you, you'll be thanking me. And begging for more.

And hopelessly in love with me."

"Never," I hissed at him in anger.

He grinned wider.

"We'll see. We'll see. Are you ready to kiss the whip?"

Made in United States
Troutdale, OR
12/30/2024